His head bent toward Camilla's, their lips only a breath apart. Kissing Camilla would be an epically bad decision, but he wasn't sure he had the strength to stop himself from making it.

"Making up after a fight has never been so fun as when making up with you."

Camilla stiffened at his words. "This is a bad idea. We've had far more than a fight. Danny, we've practically fought an emotional war. I can't…" Without another word, she spun and walked to her car. He recognized the angry set of her shoulders.

Maybe he'd taken the flirting a bit too far, since he didn't plan on following through with anything. It wouldn't be fair to her if he started something he had no intention of finishing. He wanted to put Greenbriar in his rearview as soon as the terms of the will had been fulfilled, didn't he?

What he wanted most of all in that moment was to find a way to banish that deep-seated sense of being completely and utterly alone in the world.

He had no idea where to start.

Dear Reader,

Even when a couple is in love, sometimes life gets in their way. Danny and Camilla's engagement ended and they found themselves living life separately despite being in love. Camilla never truly gave up hope that Danny would return to her life despite the pain his absence had caused her. And Danny never found anyone who filled the spot in his heart left by Camilla.

When they are pushed back together again, all the emotions and attraction from the past are still apparent. But Camilla is far more cautious now, and the reasons Danny pushed her away are still just as valid.

I think we've all had those relationships that ended where we wondered if we should give it another try, and yet sometimes the reasons why it ended remain a block. I hope you enjoy Danny and Camilla's second chance at love. Their journey to forgiveness and the spark of their rekindled love were fun to write.

Happy reading!

Allie

REUNITED WITH DOCTOR DEVEREAUX

ALLIE KINCHELOE

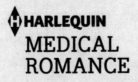

MEDICAL ROMANCE

HARLEQUIN®

MEDICAL ROMANCE™

Recycling programs
for this product may
not exist in your area.

ISBN-13: 978-1-335-40451-0

Reunited with Doctor Devereaux

Harlequin Enterprises ULC
22 Adelaide St. West, 40th Floor
Toronto, Ontario M5H 4E3, Canada
www.Harlequin.com

Printed in U.S.A.

Allie Kincheloe has been writing stories as long as she can remember, and somehow, they always become romances. Always a Kentucky girl at heart, she now lives in Tennessee with her husband, children and a growing menagerie of pets. Visit her on Twitter: @alliekauthor.

Books by Allie Kincheloe

Harlequin Medical Romance

Heart Surgeon's Second Chance
A Nurse, a Surgeon, a Christmas Engagement

Visit the Author Profile page at Harlequin.com.

To my husband and family—without your support, this book wouldn't exist.

CHAPTER ONE

AFTER EIGHT YEARS, three months, sixteen days, and—Camilla glanced up at the oversize clock on the wall of the law office—twenty-seven minutes, Danny Owens had walked back into her life. She swallowed hard.

Not that she was counting.

Counting would be stupid, considering that the last time they were together Danny had upended her entire future. So, no, she absolutely was *not* counting how long it had been since she'd seen the only man she'd ever loved. In fact, he was the last person she wanted to see, and her stomach churned as he knocked on the open office door.

Fleetingly, she thought it was good she hadn't eaten much today. If she had, the whirlwind in her stomach might have gotten the best of her.

Oh, she'd dreamed of the moment when

she'd see him again, imagining how he would look and his expression when he first saw her face. Of the time when he'd come crawling back with an apology on his lips, begging her to forgive the stupidity of his actions.

But he never had.

Seeing him now, in this way, was so much harder than she'd expected, although she'd certainly never thought it would be easy. Maybe today she'd finally get some answers on why Danny had ended their relationship so abruptly. Maybe this was fate providing her with the closure denied her for the better part of a decade.

"Dr. Owens, thank you for coming in today." The estate attorney rose from his desk and offered a hand for Danny to shake. "Now that both you and Dr. Devereaux are here, we can begin." In a crisp dark suit, Danny showed little sign that he'd been traveling. He was immaculately groomed and held himself tall, with an authority to his presence that demanded attention. Six feet one inches of firm muscle? Oh, yes, he certainly commanded her attention. Awareness buzzed through her as her eyes roamed the once familiar angles of his body, taking in the changes his time in the Army had made to his physique. The masculinity he exuded had grown stronger with the years that had passed, and despite their painful history, a deep yearning rushed over Camilla when his gaze flicked in her direction.

Heart racing like she'd just run a full marathon, Camilla made eye contact with Danny only to have him look away like she was a total stranger. She watched him in profile as he shook hands with the lawyer and settled into the leather wingback chair next to her, never once glancing her way again. Well, if she'd needed further confirmation that she'd never meant as much to him as he had to her, she'd just gotten it.

If he could push her out of his mind so easily, then she would do the same. Danny Owens wasn't going to hurt her again, because she refused to give him that power. It had taken far too many years and prayers to fix what he had broken. Two could play this game. She straightened her posture and pushed away the burst of memories that threatened to overwhelm her. There was no time for a detour into melancholia, and certainly no time to let a shared past take her down the path to future heartache.

Letting stubbornness lift her chin, Camilla turned her focus to the attorney. "Are we ready to get started here?"

"Of course, Dr. Devereaux." The attorney

shuffled a few files on his desk, opening one and putting on a pair of thick, black-rimmed reading glasses before looking up. He offered them each a sympathetic smile. "So, it can be a terrible thing, the reading of a will. Especially for someone as beloved to our town as Dr. Robert Owens."

"Yeah, yeah, we all know what a saint my father was," Danny drawled.

The gravelly quality to his voice had deepened since their last meeting. It sparked a curiosity about how else he might have changed over the years they'd been apart. No, no, no, that line of thought was forbidden. Camilla pinched her wrist. She could not go down that rabbit hole with Danny. It would only end badly for her. But keeping her mind on the conversation in front of her proved difficult as her thoughts wanted to drift off to the man sitting within arm's reach, the man she'd first given herself to, heart and soul.

"Your father was the best man I've ever known," she argued.

Robert Owens had been the only positive male role model she'd had. After bouncing from foster home to foster home for most of her formative years, she'd finally landed in a group home in Greenbriar, Kentucky. It was while attending the local high school that she'd met Danny. Then he'd brought her home to meet his parents, Robert and Linda, and his younger brother, Robby. For the first time in her life, she'd seen what a normal family dynamic looked like, warts and all.

Her early years had taught her that love was a fantasy only accessible to those with a tremendous amount of luck. And the one thing she'd most certainly never had? Luck. But Danny's gentle touch and the way he and his family had treated her, like she truly mattered, had given her hope, and so she'd finally risked opening up enough to let someone in. To fall in love.

And just look where that got you, Camilla Ann.

"To you, maybe," Danny growled out, his clenched jaw showing his displeasure.

Finally looking at her, his brown eyes flashed with an anger she was all too familiar with. Those chocolate brown eyes had always mesmerized her, tempting her close with every sparkle, but the vibe he projected now silently screamed for her to keep her distance. A lot of feelings were displayed within the intensity of his gaze—anger, grief, frustration, but nothing loving. Nothing that showed their history mattered to him in the slightest. He closed his eyes in what would seem a long blink to anyone not watching him as carefully as Camilla was, and when he looked at her again, his face could have been chiseled from stone for all the emotion he showed.

"But then again, good ol' Dad never held your past transgressions against you like he did mine. He always loved you no matter what, didn't he?"

In some ways, she'd been expecting that comment. From the moment she'd met them, Danny and Robert had butted heads at nearly every step along the line. Yet she still gaped at him in shock. Somehow, she'd expected Danny to cool the animosity now that his father was gone, but the anger radiating off him remained raw and unfazed by time.

"Ahem. Perhaps we can stick to the topic that brought us here today," the attorney interjected before Camilla could form a rebuttal to Danny's accusation. "And that is the terms of Dr. Owens's will. I have a letter from him that he wished to have read aloud today. If you are ready?"

He paused, one bushy white eyebrow raised, until both Danny and Camilla acknowledged his question with a nod. Pulling a sheet of lined yellow paper out of the file, he cleared his throat and began to read.

"'Danny, Camilla, the two of you were

my sole reasons for going on after Linda and Robby were taken from me too soon.'"

Danny stiffened next to her.

The lawyer paused for a second, but when Danny didn't speak, he continued reading. "'Have strength today, although I know how hard it is to say goodbye. Know that you were both deeply loved, and lean on each other as you grieve, but do not grieve for long. Life is far too short to spend time lost in the memories of the past.'"

Camilla could hear the words in Robert's deep baritone, as if he were sitting right there, speaking the words to them directly. Closing her eyes, she pictured his kind face. It was only a few days ago that she'd sat by his side, holding his hand while he took his final breaths. *Oh, Robert, how I will miss you!*

"'Danny, my dearest son, I may not have said it enough in life, but I couldn't help taking this last opportunity to tell you just how proud you have made me. Although I didn't agree with your decision to join the Army, you were right that it was your choice to make. Go forward in life with the fortitude your time in service has instilled in you. To you, my boy, I leave the lake house and all its contents. So many of my fondest memories of your childhood were made on the shores of that lake. It is my hope that someday, standing on the dock there and looking out over the water will fill you with as much peace as it did me.'"

The lawyer took a sip of water before continuing.

"'My cherished Camilla, you filled a void in my life only a daughter could, and these last months have only been possible as a result of your dedication to my care. I hope that you know how much you were loved and appreciated by this lonely old man. Take that knowledge into your future with an open heart. Be willing to take a chance when love comes your way again. To you, child of my heart, I leave the house on Maple Street and all its contents. Turn that house into the home it once was and is meant to be again. Fill it with children, laughter, and above all—love.'"

Danny scoffed, his mask of indifference slipping momentarily. "Of course, he leaves you my childhood home and I get a shack on the lake. Even in death, he's still punishing me for defying him."

"It's hardly a shack." She rolled her eyes at his grumbling. While the lake house was smaller than the house, Robert had renovated it a few years back to a high-quality standard. Given Danny's avoidance of Greenbriar, though, he probably had no clue what his father had done to it. If Danny wanted to sell it, then he'd have no problems getting a good price for it. But rather than continue to argue that point, she'd let him discover for himself what a gem he'd inherited.

"What about the medical practice?" Danny asked.

Holding her breath, Camilla awaited that answer. This was the part of Robert's estate she'd been waiting to hear about.

"I wasn't finished." The attorney waved the letter, his impatience with Danny's interruptions starting to show. He cleared his throat and continued to read. "'It is my last wish that the two of you will find your way back to each other, despite the years, despite the physical and emotional distances between you. Forgive an old man this last chance to meddle in the affairs of his loved ones, but I had to try. I conditionally leave Greenbriar Medical Clinic, both the building and the practice, to the both of you. You will run it together for the next six months and own it jointly at the end of that time. However, if you refuse to abide by the terms of this will, the clinic will be dissolved, liquidated, and any proceeds diverted to various military-connected charities, as well as the Greenbriar group home.'"

With her heart sinking all the way to her feet, Camilla stood and went to the window. She stared across the town square to the aging brick building that held the medical practice where she'd worked for most of her medical career. The sharp stab of what could only be labeled as betrayal cut through her. Day in and day out, she'd worked side by side with Robert. First as his employee, then later with the expectation that one day she would be a partner or take over when he retired. Robert had never said outright that he would leave the practice solely to her, but he'd strongly implied it.

Robert had known that she wanted—no, *needed*—to stay in Greenbriar, and their conversations had led her to believe that the clinic would be hers upon his death. He'd been more aware than anyone how badly Danny had destroyed her. His shoulder had been the one she'd cried on. They'd grieved together. He'd stood by her when she'd picked up the shattered pieces of her heart and stuck them back together with stubbornness and a little duct tape. Robert had been the only one who saw the depths of her pain. How could he put her future in the hands of a man who had already abandoned her once?

She took a deep breath and blinked away

her fears. Now was not the time for that line of thinking. She had to find the strength that had carried her through those dark days and kept her moving forward. She would not let Danny Owens take away her future again.

Come on, Camilla. Pull it together. No tears. If you survived years of foster homes and having your heart marched across by Danny, you can handle six months working next to him.

She'd simply set a schedule where they didn't have to see each other on a daily basis and cross the days off on the calendar like she used to whenever she moved into a new home. But instead of counting up to see if any new home would break the record length of one hundred and forty-three days, she'd count down the one hundred and eighty days until Danny was gone from her life once more. She would get through this, like she'd gotten through every other hard time in her life, and when Danny left once again to go back to his, she'd continue on like he'd never shown his face here in her town.

"You're telling me that if I want to inherit my father's medical practice, I have to move back to a town that doesn't even qualify for a map dot for the next six months? I have commitments I can't fulfill if I'm stuck here in the middle of nowhere." Tight with anger, Danny's voice held a no-nonsense tone that demanded a reply.

"The terms of the will are set," the attorney confirmed. While he didn't cower at Danny's growling, the attorney looked uncomfortable. His eyes flicked toward the door as if he were getting ready to run out of his own office to avoid further confrontation.

"I'm not exactly jumping for joy at the thought of spending the next six months with you, either, Danny," Camilla said over her shoulder. Leaning her head against the window frame, she fought to regain her composure. She hugged her arms tight around her body, desperately trying to combat the creeping fear encasing her soul. The uncertainty of having her future in Danny's hands chilled her to the core, but she would not let him see how badly his presence upset her. "I've worked hard for this practice. I know the patients and their conditions. I have been on call for years so that your father could rest, and I took over entirely when his health deteriorated. I expected—"

"You expected him to just hand you the keys to a house and a profitable medical practice," Danny interrupted.

She spun around at the harsh accusation he threw at her. "I did no such thing!"

Hot stinging behind her eyelids reminded her of when she'd tripped and fallen flat on her face on her first day in a new school. That had been the last time she'd cried in public, too. She blinked hard, praying that the tears would stay where they belonged. She had come to this will reading with very little expectation, and for Danny to say otherwise was unfair.

"Come on, Camilla, what'd you think was gonna happen here today? You'd get everything even though he was *my* father?" Danny folded his arms over his chest and his suit jacket pulled tight across his broad shoulders. The straight set of his spine and the rigidity of his posture must have come from his time in the military, because the boy she'd loved had never been so solid. His sharp glare would wither a weaker person, but she had been through far too much in her life to shrink away from anything he could dish out. "Is it cutting to your core that you didn't get the lake house, too?"

"No," she asserted, standing up straight and facing him head-on. "I thought he'd leave me the practice and leave everything else to you. And if you truly think otherwise, then it's a good thing you and I didn't work out, because you clearly don't know me at all."

The thought that Robert would leave her everything had never even been a blip on her radar. The house was unexpected—very much welcome, but unexpected, nonetheless. She'd been renting the large, two-story home from Robert since he'd moved into the remodeled lakeside cottage when he'd gotten sick and stairs were too difficult for him to manage. That house was the only place she'd ever really considered a home and for Robert to have recognized that fact touched her heart, but she'd certainly never even hoped that he'd leave her anything more than the clinic she'd worked so hard for.

"Ahem. The letter continues, if I may," the attorney interjected, silencing any further argument. "'Here's where I'll say, quiet your protests. I know the two of you very well, so I'm sure you've both just had a moment. There may have been some yelling or even tears, but the time for that has gone. Find peace with my decision and know that it was made with your best interests at heart. Family is the most important thing in this life. Never forget that. And never forget just how much you were both loved. Now I'll say goodbye.'"

The attorney refolded the paper and laid it

back on the file. Pulling his glasses off, he squeezed the bridge of his nose. His attitude screamed that he'd aged a decade in the reading of that letter. "Now, you can contest the will, but doing that will just take longer than the six months you two would need to work together."

"Does the six-month period have to begin immediately or can I have a few weeks to get things settled away from Greenbriar? I have commitments, a job. People are counting on me."

Camilla snorted. "Your father counted on you and you weren't here."

Danny closed his eyes and sucked in a deep breath, trying to calm the storm of emotions rushing over him. All he managed to do was get a lungful of Camilla's familiar, sweet perfume. The soft floral scent permeated his being and stoked memories of times best left forgotten.

As if he could ever forget her.

Trust his old man to take one more stab at righting what he'd seen as one of Danny's biggest mistakes. His father had never forgiven him for pushing Camilla away, but what Robert Owens hadn't known was that ending things with Camilla had been the only way Danny could think of to protect her.

And now, thanks to his father, he was tied back to the town he couldn't wait to leave, and had to spend the next six months working with *her*. The very idea of them working peacefully side by side for an extended period of time was laughable. He'd spent eight years in the Army, some of that time in a combat zone; he'd watched people he loved die right in front of him, and the idea of spending one hundred and eighty days at Camilla's side scared him more than anything ever had.

She'd been his everything once. They'd planned to conquer the world together, or at least this one little corner of it. They were going to get their bachelor's degrees together, then go to med school, and then come back to Greenbriar and take over his dad's medical practice. Only part of that plan materialized when they'd been unable to get into the same medical school. Despite that hiccup, they'd stayed as close as possible through medical schools on opposite ends of the country. Then, in the blink of an eye, everything had changed. His mother and brother had been killed in an accident and he'd been behind the wheel.

When Camilla had shown up in his hospital room, he'd sent her away, filled with self-loathing and guilt. Ending things with her had been the hardest thing he'd ever done. He'd broken her heart because he knew he was no good for her. He'd been no good to anyone at that point, even himself.

But in the process, he'd broken his own heart, too. And now they had to coexist in a work environment made hostile entirely through his own efforts.

Fantastic.

Danny had a strong suspicion that his dad had guessed how difficult it would be for him to work side by side with Camilla and had probably done it to push him out of his comfort zone. His dad had never given up hope that Danny would "come to his senses" and beg for Camilla's forgiveness. This stunt was just a last try to push them back together. Even in death, the old man wouldn't relent.

"Dad never told me how sick he was," he argued. If he had known, he would definitely have made more of an attempt to come home sooner, to rebuild those bridges he'd burned with such enthusiasm on his way out of town. At least the ones with his father... He should have made time to visit when he'd processed out of the Army, rather than going straight to Boston and jumping right into his job there as an attending in the emergency department. But his dad had kept his health struggles tightly under wraps and hadn't let a sliver of information come out that would have clued Danny in to the cancer poisoning his father's organs. He'd only found out two days ago, when his dad's oncologist had called to tell him that his father was at peace, his suffering now over, and it was time to come home to lay his body to rest.

He'd had two days to come to terms with his father's death and it still felt unreal. He kept expecting his dad to walk through the door, gruffly saying, "What kinda son makes a man fake his own death just to get him to visit?" Man, he wished it had all been a joke. What he wouldn't give to hug his old man just one more time. He squeezed his hand into a fist and resisted the urge to slam it into the wood paneling lining the office. He hadn't gotten to say goodbye.

"Well, if you'd visited him anytime in the last two years, you would have seen it for yourself." Even when she called him to task for his transgressions, Camilla's voice was low and even. Her unique ability to maintain this soft and steady tone had never failed to impress him. The coldness in her eyes told him she hadn't forgiven him—not for the words he'd hurled at her that still haunted his soul, or his absence since that fateful day. Some wounds not even time could heal.

Not that he blamed her. He knew he'd given her something she'd never had—love and acceptance—and then snatched it away from her in that hospital room. In one cruel moment, he'd stolen years of hard-won progress from her. Her background had taught her that "love" meant someone wanted something from you. It had taken a lot of time and coaxing for her to open up to him and he'd stomped all over her trust, even kicking dirt into the wounds. What he had done to her was unforgivable.

"Camilla, I..." He trailed off. Every word he thought of saying sat heavy on his tongue, refusing to roll off into another lie. He'd lied to her enough. If nothing else, she deserved his honesty today. "Okay, you're right. I was a lousy son."

He looked away, not wanting to see the judgment in her eyes. As a sixteen-year-old boy, he'd fallen head over heels with the beautiful girl from the group home whose mismatched clothes never fit properly, but who had so much sass that she kept him on his toes. He'd promised her the world. It was a resolution he'd been unable to keep, unfortunately.

After he'd broken so many promises to her, he couldn't bear to look her in the eye. Not coming home had made it easier to avoid Camilla. Staying away allowed him to minimize the drama he assumed he'd find if he set foot in Greenbriar. He'd created a cocoon around himself that kept everyone at a distance, even the people he saw on a daily basis. But in protecting himself, he'd missed his father's final days.

One thing he couldn't avoid, though, was the guilt. He hadn't been there when his father needed him. He was a doctor, after all, so he should have heard in his father's voice how sick he was. There should have been something audible that told him the man was dying, but even in their final conversation last week, his dad had sounded the same to him as he always had. He'd asked for Danny to come home like always, lectured him again about the choices he'd made that had carried Danny away from Greenbriar and Camilla, but he'd ended the call with the same brusque "Love you, son." Like every phone call they'd had in the last eight years.

Why hadn't his dad told him he was sick?

Why hadn't his dad given him the opportunity to truly make things right between them?

Why was Camilla even more beautiful than the day he'd broken off their three-year engagement?

Inhaling deeply, he shoved that thought back into the box of memories he kept locked away in the dark recesses of his mind. He couldn't relive the day he'd broken their hearts or revise the inner turmoil that he still struggled to shake.

He shifted his weight and let the pain of seeing her again wash over him. Eight years and it still hurt. Today he savored that pain, though, because the angry ache pulled him into the present and gave him something to focus on. It was a welcome distraction from the crushing emotions threatening to pull him under.

"I think asking for a couple weeks to settle your current affairs out of town is a reasonable request, and I see no reason why that can't be accommodated." The attorney pulled a blank notepad out and grabbed a pen. "How does beginning on February first sound to the two of you? Then the six-month time frame can end on August first."

Camilla murmured her assent.

Danny nodded. He could only hope that

the administration at the hospital where he worked would be willing to let him out of his contract this soon. Maybe when he explained the circumstances, they'd be understanding. He'd only been a civilian for three months and already he was going to have to ask for concessions from an administration who eyed him warily at best.

Danny blew out a breath. It wasn't like he had many options. His dad had backed him into a corner, and after all the pain he'd caused in the past, Danny couldn't take the clinic from Camilla now. He was sure his father had banked on the fact that he'd realize she was the one who'd be hurt if the clinic had to close and that there'd be enough lingering love, or guilt, left inside him to keep him from rejecting the terms of the will and forcing the sale of the clinic.

The attorney jotted down some notes on the yellow paper. "I'll get this formalized for you both to sign. There are also a few signatures I'll need for the transfer of property from each of you."

Before any of them said another word, the door opened and slammed hard into the wall. Danny jumped at the sudden noise, heart racing. He had to force himself to breathe when his brain clued him in that there was no immediate danger and he waited for the adrenaline spike to ease. Even after being stateside for well over a year now, sudden noises still threw him back to his time in the war zone and the fear he'd felt as bullets whizzed past his ear.

The young woman who had burst into the office spoke in a rush, the words tumbling past her lips with barely a pause for breath. "Dr. Devereaux, Caden's having a lot of trouble breathing. I didn't know if it was safe to drive him all the way out to the emergency room, and they said it would be forty-five minutes before the ambulance could get out here because there's a big accident up on the highway."

In her arms she carried a small boy, maybe four years old, who was wheezing loud enough that Danny could hear the gasps from across the room. His mind sought to diagnose, beginning with the thought of asthma.

Before he could put voice to that, though, Camilla was already ushering them back out the door. "Let's get him over to the office and get him a breathing treatment. Have you given him his inhaler today?"

Their voices faded as they walked away.

With a quick glance at the attorney, Danny followed them out of the office. His gaze moved over the downtown area as he crossed from the attorney's office. The sleepy Southern town was cold this time of year. Dreary and dull, with the only action being the old men driving around the square in their pickups. When it was warm, they'd take up residence on the stone wall in front of the courthouse with their chewing tobacco and empty bottles to spit in. There was no coffee shop on the corner to get a caffeine jolt, just a single diner where the old women of the town occupied half the booths and gossiped about the old men.

If it weren't for the movement of the trucks, someone might think the town had been abandoned years ago. None of the vehicles within sight were current models and several looked to be as old as the buildings surrounding the square, including Danny's father's medical practice.

Stepping through those clinic doors was like stepping back into his childhood, though, and took his thoughts from the town that never changed to the grief of a son now orphaned. The hideous faded floral wallpaper his mother had picked out when he was a child still graced the walls but was now faded, and memories of her excitement at finding what she'd considered the perfect pattern fluttered through his mind. Other than the shiny new computer sitting at the reception desk, everything was exactly as he remembered.

A large picture of his parents hung on the back wall. Their thirtieth anniversary, he recalled. They'd never made it to thirty-one. His mom had passed away three months later. His brother, too.

He still took the long way into Greenbriar to avoid driving that stretch of road. And now his dad was gone, too. He swallowed hard, trying to shake the feeling of being at home for the first time in so long. To shake away the guilt that had settled back on his shoulders when he'd passed the city limits sign.

The only way to get through this was to focus on all the things he'd hated about Greenbriar. He couldn't afford to get sucked into the nostalgia and any comfort he might find here. While he needed to call somewhat of a truce with Camilla, he also had to make sure that she knew reconciliation wasn't an option—not that he was too worried about that last. The ice daggers she'd been shooting from her eyes ever since he'd arrived had showed no sign of thawing.

But he had to remove any temptation.

It was going to be a balancing act, for sure. He'd have to be nice enough to maintain the peace, but enough of a jerk that she didn't soften toward him. He took a deep breath and fortified his resolve. He'd faced down insurgents with semiautomatic weapons; a petite doctor with skin as soft as velvet shouldn't be too hard.

Stepping into the hallway, he looked into the first exam room and quickly moved past it to the second. There he found Camilla with the young mother and child. Camilla was setting up a nebulizer.

"Are you giving him albuterol?" he asked. The standard medication used to treat an asthma attack, albuterol was often given via a nebulizer like the one Camilla had in her hands. It would have been his first step, too, if the kid's lungs sounded as bad as his breathing indicated.

She glanced up at him briefly before opening a small vial of medication and pouring it into a chamber on the tubing. She slipped the mask over the child's face and turned the machine on before giving him an answer. "You know that I am."

"Steroids, too?"

Camilla nodded. "That's the plan."

"I'd grab them for you, but I don't have access to the medication cabinet."

"It's fine," Camilla muttered to him. She

laid a hand on the mother's arm. "I'm going to step out and talk to Dr. Owens in the hallway."

"Dr. Owens?" The young woman looked confused. "But I thought…"

"I'm his son Danny," he said, hoping to clarify things for her. She looked vaguely familiar, like most of the people in this town, but he couldn't seem to come up with her name.

"I'll be back in just a moment to check on Caden." Camilla smiled softly at the worried mother and then turned to him, and that softness disappeared into a harsh frown. "I'm going to fetch those steroids and get them into him. If you would…" She waved a hand toward his father's office across the hall.

He stepped through the open door. Another intense wave of grief rushed over him when he stood in front of the antique walnut desk his father had kept polished to a shine. He ran a finger across the dark, gleaming surface.

Why didn't you give me the chance to say goodbye to you, old man? Did you hate me that much?

"What are you doing here, Danny? I am perfectly capable of taking care of a child with asthma. I don't require the assistance of a big-city trauma surgeon." Camilla crossed her arms over her chest and his gaze flicked down to the hint of cleavage her blouse revealed. Immediately adjusting her clothing, she hissed out, "Keep your eyes on my face and your thoughts to a PG rating, please."

"Maybe I just wanted to check out my inheritance," he snapped, trying to regain the high ground with her. He knew he couldn't afford to let his guard down, but even so, the baldness of those words sat hard on his heart. Maybe it was the heartbreak he glimpsed in her eyes before she shut down and the emotionless facade of their teen years returned to her gaze. But it was too late by that point to retract the words; the harm had been done. "That came out badly."

He was the one who had hurt her. She had done nothing but love him and she certainly had the right to be suspicious of his motives now. He'd given her plenty of reason. He'd broken her heart because he knew he wasn't good enough for her. He'd been of no use to anyone, even himself. So, why was he acting so defensively toward her?

Guilt, maybe? His mom had always said, *A guilty conscious will stalk you for the rest of your life*. If this wasn't proof of that…

Tilting her head, Camilla scrutinized him. He tried not to let her see what he was feeling, but her time in foster care had made her an expert at decoding faces. She'd always been able to read him like a book, while he'd struggled to name a single emotion from her. She'd kept her feelings close to the chest, burying things so deep he wasn't sure she even processed them.

When they'd first started dating, he'd tried to get her to open up to him about her past, to discover details about her childhood, but she had shut that line of questioning down fast. Even when they'd been together long enough for her to trust him, there were things she still refused to share, topics that he couldn't touch without her walking away.

Camilla had a policy that the past was the past and it had no place in her present or future. Knowing that, his last words to her eight years ago had been cold, cruel, and designed to cut straight to her core—the only way he knew how to protect her from himself.

He still hated himself for using that knowledge to his advantage.

In doing so, he had put himself in the position of being her past, and despite being forced together for the foreseeable future, there had never been more distance between them.

CHAPTER TWO

"I HAVE A PATIENT. I don't have time for—" she motioned between them "—whatever you are trying to do here."

Danny stared at her, his gaze searching. "We need to bury the past if we are going to get through this ridiculous condition my father has put on us. You think you can do that? Or should we just tell that lawyer to prepare the clinic for sale?"

Camilla pressed a fist to her mouth. She'd poured her heart and soul into this clinic, yes, but Danny had grown up here. Yet he could talk so callously of disposing of it, like it meant absolutely nothing. Sadness settled over her, burdening her already grieving heart.

Did the man really not have any emotional connection to this town or this clinic?

Or me?

"No, I do not want to prepare the clinic for

sale!" Her hands clenched at her sides and she fought down the urge to punch something. *Or someone.* She took a deep, calming breath before she continued her argument. "You may have another job to go back to, but this is it for me. I painted those exam rooms myself. I scrubbed down the wallpaper in the lobby when your father refused to let me replace it. I will not give this place up without a fight."

He lifted one shoulder in a casual shrug. "My mom picked out that wallpaper. Dad was probably being sentimental about it."

"Well, then you'll forgive me for being sentimental about wanting to hang on to *my* clinic." Being in Danny's presence made her feel exposed in a way she hadn't felt in years. She'd thought she had prepared herself for the emotional uproar that seeing him again would evoke, but she wasn't ready. She had practiced things to say. She'd memorized a few witty lines that she might use as comebacks to his verbal attacks, but now that they were face-to-face, those rehearsed words refused to come. The words she did manage to eke out revealed a weakness that she hated letting him hear.

Oh, and he definitely heard the quiver in her voice, because his gaze softened and his hand twitched in her direction like he might reach for her. But he stayed himself before allowing that tiny movement to become a full-on action.

As a kid, she'd learned to have a thick skin. It was a talent she'd developed through years of foster care, along with the ability to suss out the tiniest of reactions in a person's expression—like that hint of indication he wanted to comfort her. She couldn't let her guard down around him again, though. With a deep, stabilizing breath, Camilla locked down her emotions. No one got past her defenses if she didn't allow them to, and that mantra had kept her safe. She'd learned early the importance of protecting herself, and that lesson had been reinforced incredibly painfully by the man standing in front of her.

"It's that important to you?" he asked. He ran his fingers through his short hair. With a huff of disbelief, he continued, "You could move anywhere. Start your own practice in the city where people wouldn't try to pay you with chickens."

She rolled her eyes at his snarky comment. "Greenbriar is a small town, but it's not so backwoods that anyone has ever attempted to pay me in livestock. You know I made promises to the people of this town, Danny. They paid to put me through medical school. They upheld their end of the bargain and I'm still trying to uphold mine."

She'd honored the commitment to come back to Greenbriar and practice after the town had collected money to provide a scholarship fund for her. The small town had embraced her like a long-lost daughter and given her a much-wanted sense of family and community. She would not turn her back on that, even if that meant she started her own practice from scratch in her living room.

Danny gave an almost imperceptible shake of his head. His lips—lips she'd once lived to kiss—narrowed to nothing more than a slash. "I doubt they intended you to devote your entire life to this one-horse town."

For Danny, Greenbriar had been a prison that stifled his adventurous soul. He'd loved every minute of getting out of town for college and medical school. Camilla, however, had longed to put down roots. His upbringing had given him a stability that allowed him to take risks, while hers had made her desperate for the security of the familiar.

"We have three horses now, I'll have you know." She tried to lighten the conversation since there was still a patient in the building who didn't need to be subjected to the verbal brawl that would inevitably result from the two of them hashing out their differences. "And I have a patient to check on."

As she stepped past Danny, he reached a hand out and let his fingers brush against her wrist. "We have to talk about this."

The skin he'd touched burned like fire had kissed it. She couldn't stop the gasp that escaped her at the contact. Flexing the hand, she tried to shake away the red-hot desire that ghost of a touch had spurred. Her body still responded to Danny, desperately wanting his touch, even if her heart raced in fear of being shattered again and her brain argued that logically, getting involved with a man who had already left her once was an incredibly bad idea.

She set her jaw and drew on the memory of their last meeting to give her strength. The reminder of how Danny had tossed her out of his hospital room after pulling the engagement ring off her finger was enough to secure her resolve. Even years later, the words he'd spit out still haunted her, creating doubt in every relationship she'd had since. Oh, she'd tried to put them out of her mind and move on, but his dismissal had been so harsh and definite that she'd given up dating altogether for years. If a man who'd claimed she was the love of his life could toss her aside like a wet newspaper, how could she ever trust a stranger?

Camilla straightened her spine. "I have a patient," she reiterated, forcing herself to move away from him and take the few steps across the hall. She tapped lightly on the exam room door and let herself back in.

Hoping that the fragile state of her emotions wasn't showing, she washed her hands and tried to pull herself together. Her patient needed—deserved—a focused doctor and she was going to give him one. Danny Owens had taken a lot from her, but she would not relinquish her professionalism.

"How's it coming along?"

Caden's mother shook the little medication chamber and very little remained. "Looks like it's about done. His breathing doesn't sound quite as labored. At least not to me, but it could be wishful thinking."

Flipping the nebulizer off, Camilla eased the mask from Caden's face. His lips were still as blue as they were before starting the albuterol treatment.

Camilla clipped the pulse-ox monitor to his tiny index finger and put her stethoscope to use as she listened to the child's chest. With her eyes closed, she focused on the sound of his breathing. Even with the albuterol treatment, he wasn't moving air as much as she would like. The good news was that Caden's chest wasn't completely silent. He was still moving some air, just not enough. His oxygen levels had risen only a single point.

"How are you feeling, Caden?" she asked.

The preschooler's nostrils flared in time with his still-labored breathing, his abdominal muscles rising with each struggling breath. "Hurts," he said on a gasp, waving one hand at his chest.

"It hurts to breathe?" Camilla asked.

Caden only nodded.

"The steroids and albuterol should have started doing something," Danny said from the doorway.

"Thank you, Dr. Obvious," she muttered under her breath. It was as if Danny had forgotten that she also had a medical degree. She bit back the harsher retort tempting her tongue.

"Let's do another albuterol treatment."

Caden's mom cuddled the boy close and ran her hand up and down his back. "What if that doesn't work?"

Camilla smiled at the gentle gesture of comfort. "We are going to think positive. Caden is going to need to go to the hospital tonight, though. I think it's best we keep him monitored and on oxygen. Let's have him see a respiratory specialist, too."

The other woman nodded slowly.

Danny brought in the second dose of albuterol, handing it over without a word. He must have found his dad's keys to the medication locker, Camilla thought. She took the little vial from his outstretched hands carefully to avoid another brush of her skin against his.

She extended a hint of an olive branch. "Do you want to listen to his lungs and see if you agree with my plan, Dr. Owens?"

Danny took the stethoscope from around Camilla's neck gently. The sharing of the equipment held an intimacy Camilla had not expected. She readied the nebulizer for the second dose of medication and tried to still her shaking hands.

"Okay, Caden, one more round of this yucky medicine. And hopefully then you can breathe without hurting." She reaffixed the mask to his face and smoothed a hand over Caden's baby-soft hair. The urge for a child of her own rose up, as it did each time she had a very young patient.

Someday, she promised herself.

The second round of medication perked Caden up some. "Better," he said, still strug-

gling to speak in words. Phrases seemed beyond him.

Danny leaned over him, listening again
to his lungs. Camilla wanted to snatch her
stethoscope back so that she could hear for
herself what progress the medication had
given him, but forced herself to wait. Professionals didn't snatch equipment away from
their colleagues.

Finally, Danny handed the stethoscope
over. "There's still significant intercostal and
substernal retractions. Pan-expiratory and in-
spiratory wheezes strongly present, although
diminished some from the level prior to albuterol administration." His tone was clipped,
clinical. "I agree with your assessment that
hospital monitoring tonight would be pru-
dent."

"Thank you, Dr. Owens," she said as she
took the proffered equipment. She put the
stethoscope to her ears and listened to Caden's heart and lungs. Given that he'd had
two subsequent doses of albuterol, his elevated heart rate was expected. His lungs did
sound quite a bit better than when he'd first
arrived in her office, but there was far too
much distress remaining for her to feel comfortable sending him home.

Draping the stethoscope around her neck,

she told the boy's mother, "Definitely think it is the best thing for Caden if we send him over to Children's to be monitored overnight. I know it's a bit of a drive, but I don't think going home is the best course of action. He's going to need albuterol treatments all through the night. And I'd really like them to keep an eye on his O2 saturation, as well. I'm going to send all his information over to the hospital. You head on over there and they should, hopefully, have a room ready for you by the time you get there." She smiled at Caden. "And I'll come by first thing in the morning to check on you."

"Thanks, Dr. Devereaux. We'll see you in the morning." The mother helped the boy into his coat before they left the exam room with a final wave.

Camilla typed in all her care instructions so that they'd be available to the hospital staff when Caden arrived. Since she'd never sent Caden to Children's and had no record of hospital stays in his chart, she sent over all the pertinent details, as well, choosing to err on the side of caution and provide more information on the off chance it was needed.

With that done, Camilla walked out to the lobby and took down the sign she'd taped to the door stating she'd be at the attorney's office that afternoon. She replaced it with the regular after-hours sign with her phone number in bold print.

"You were really good with him," Danny said from behind her, causing her to jump as he startled her. He'd been so quiet that she'd thought he might have left.

"What did you expect? That I'd be cold and unfeeling? I'm afraid I reserve that demeanor for only very special people." She filled her voice with as much ice as she could muster and could barely contain her delight when the barb struck home.

"Ouch." Danny winced. "No, I just meant that I hadn't thought you would be that good with children."

"Keep digging, Danny, just keep digging."

Why wouldn't she be good with children? Just because she hadn't had a proper family didn't mean she hadn't had more than her share of experience taking care of children. A lot of the foster homes she'd been in had only wanted a teen girl to help look after the younger children. She'd changed as many diapers as any parent had. Anyway, he knew she wanted a family someday. Kids had always been part of her plan, a plan that once upon a time he had been on board with.

She looked at him, trying to gauge his

frame of mind and the meaning behind his words in case she was simply reading too much into his words because of their past. Although his countenance had matured since their last meeting, there was still so much that was familiar to her in the lines of his face. His thick dark hair was clipped shorter now than he'd kept it in his premilitary days. There were new shadows darkening his eyes, but the curve of his lips remained the same. He seemed taller now than before, but she thought that might be attributed to the stiffness in his posture. The more she looked at him, though, the stronger the vibe between them got and she had to look away first.

"It was actually a compliment," he grumbled.

She stomped past him, tossing her reply over her shoulder. "It didn't sound like one."

She felt, rather than heard, him follow her back into the exam room. Ripping the paper covering off the exam table, she crumpled it into a ball and shoved it roughly in the trash. He had only been back in her life for one measly hour and already she was responding to his presence in more ways than she was comfortable with.

"Wish that was my head?" he asked quietly, tossing the used mask and tubing away.

"Maybe," she allowed, her lips turning up in the barest hint of a smile. She grabbed the disinfectant and started rubbing down the exam table.

Danny let out a quick bark of laughter. "No maybes about it. Don't think I don't remember that you clean when you're angry. You can be honest about the fact that you hate my guts and would rather kick me than look at me. It will make the next six months go a lot smoother if we can be honest with each other."

She paused her movements and looked up at him. "You want honesty?"

"Yes."

Raising an eyebrow at him, she sought confirmation. "Are you sure you can handle it?"

He stepped out of the room and she almost laughed at the absurdity of him asking for honesty and leaving before she could say anything else. She scrubbed at the table harder than necessary, trying to ease some of her frustration.

"I do want honesty from you. Even if it hurts. And I hope that I can be honest with you, as well." Danny stood in the door, broom and dustpan in hand. "I figure we can start this partnership by giving this office a good

cleaning, and if you want, something of a re-
model. It's stuck in decades past."

"It may be a little dated, but it is clean." She
bristled at the implication that she'd allow the
clinic to be less than hygienic. How low was
his opinion of her if he could think she'd run
a dirty medical practice?

"That's not what I meant." Danny held a
hand up to stifle her objections. "Can we start
again, please? I promise you, every word out
of my mouth is not meant to be a criticism."

After examining the expression on his face
and seeing only honesty, she nodded slowly.

"Okay, good. Here's the thing. I have a life
away from Greenbriar. I never intended to
move back here, but now I don't exactly have
a choice."

"Not my problem."

He closed his eyes and she saw the frustration he was trying to squash. His next words
were slow and followed the grinding of his
teeth. "I'm trying here, Camilla. I think if we
could maybe agree to some ground rules, it
would help."

"Okay," she agreed cautiously. She was no
longer confident in her ability to read him
correctly. Instinctively, she wanted to believe him, but her instincts had failed her with
Danny in the past.

"Earlier I was a little harsh with you about my father giving you so much. I had no right to complain about what he chose to do with his estate, and you were right that you've been the one here day in and day out. You cared for him when he refused to even tell me he was sick. You've put the work into this town and this practice. You've earned it in a way that I never wanted to do."

She nodded slowly. His expressions said he was genuine, but she wasn't sure where he was heading with this conversation.

"Okay, so I have to be here until August. We have to make this work for six months, right? Well, how would you like to buy out my half of this practice then?"

The offer to sell her his half of the clinic at the end of the six-month period had slipped out without a lot of thought. He pressed his lips together tightly, almost needing to drag the words back and consider that proposition for a moment. His parents had poured years of time and attention into building this medical practice with his dad as the town doctor and his mom working at his side as his nurse. His dad had been so proud of his work in the community and had always hoped Danny or Robby would come home to take over when he retired. Unfortunately, neither of his parents made it to retirement, so that part of the dream would never come true. Robby hadn't even made it out of college. Danny swallowed hard, shoving down the guilt and the grief.

If he sold out, it would be like trashing his parents' dream. So he had to ask himself, did he actually *want* to sell his father's practice?

Camilla pressed forward, leaving him no time to examine his initial idea of stepping away from the clinic. "And then what? You'll sell the lake house and leave town forever?"

"Hadn't thought that far ahead," he said with a shrug.

Maybe he'd keep the lake house as a vacation home. The idea of having a secluded spot where he could leave the city and reconnect with nature certainly appealed. Being on the lake was one of the few things he had missed about Greenbriar. He could go to the ocean, yes, but he'd always been more of a tranquil lake guy. And that cottage was the last physical connection he had with his parents—letting go of it wouldn't be an easy thing to do.

"Well, this is the first time you've been back to Greenbriar since you left, so it might be best if you just made a clean break." Camilla wrapped her arms around herself, tightly.

Self-armoring for whatever she planned to say next? "We were never enough for you, were we?"

A fresh wave of guilt rushed up over him. Despite knowing his reasons for leaving her were solid, Danny knew she'd felt abandoned. He'd known she would feel that way before he ended their engagement, and while he stood by the decision being the right one, seeing just how deeply he'd wounded her in the process hurt. The pain he'd caused them both still left a raw, gaping wound on his soul.

Some nights he lay in the dark, staring up at the ceiling, and wondered what would have happened if he'd let her in back then. If he'd told her just how badly he was hurting, how her unwavering positivity felt like she was pushing him beneath the surface to drown in his own pain, would she have backed off a bit and stood by his side through it all? Camilla was one of the strongest women he'd ever met, but would she have been strong enough to weather all the nightmares he'd suffered? The flashbacks and the panic attacks that came with the terrible memories of what he'd done? Could she have looked him in the eye again, if he'd told her the complete truth?

Time had given him the distance and maturity to see that Camilla's gung ho peppiness had been a cover for her own fear and grief. Trying to explain everything to her now would only seem like excuses, though, wouldn't it? Was there anything he could say that would ease the pain she clearly still felt? Would she even believe him? He struggled to find the right words. "Camilla…"

"It's okay." The weak smile she flashed his direction said otherwise. "I don't want to bring up old grievances."

Grievances? That was how she was going to refer to their past?

"In the spirit of honesty, I think we need to." He swept the last of the dust from the floor into the dustpan and propped the broom against the wall. Turning to face her, he offered the closest thing to an apology that he could bring himself to utter. "I hurt you and there are still raw edges there that we need to smooth over so that we can both move on."

She snorted, a derisive little sound. "That's a pretty massive understatement. You more than hurt me. You ripped my heart out when you snatched my engagement ring off my finger. And when you told me that you'd never really loved me? That destroyed me."

"That wasn't…"

"I believe your exact words were, 'I don't

know why you ever thought your love would be enough for me. You were simply the best option available.' So, go ahead. Explain to me what else you could have meant."

"I didn't mean to…" Sucking in a deep breath, he tried to think of a way to justify the choices he'd made that day in a way she'd understand. He knew Camilla well enough to know that telling her he'd broken up with her for her own good wouldn't go well. He finally settled on a somewhat sanitized version of the truth. "When I ended our engagement, I was miserable, and I wanted everyone around me to share in that misery. You were so…in my face with positivity, my own personal cheerleader, when what I needed was time to mourn the loss of—" he swallowed hard "—my mother, my brother, and in a way my father. All I really wanted was to regain control of my life. And I just couldn't, so I took it out on the people around me. You bore the brunt of my pain."

It was mostly true, anyway.

"Are you saying that you think I played a part in you dumping me?" Her eyes narrowed at him. "I certainly didn't ask to be thrown out of your life without any warning."

Danny sighed. He'd said more than he

meant to and once again caused Camilla pain. This was exactly why he kept his distance from her. Everything he did, everything he said, somehow jabbed that knife right back into her heart. This right here was why he pushed people away.

If he didn't let anyone close, he couldn't hurt them.

"I know you had the best of intentions, and I know I should have just talked to you about how I was feeling. I'm the world's biggest jerk. At the time, though, that felt impossible, and I needed breathing room. But I was in the wrong headspace to have a rational conversation with you about you being so positive. I didn't need a cheerleader. I needed a shoulder to cry on. And I could only see one path through—being alone and focusing all my attention on myself. It was selfish, but it's the truth."

Every time he opened his mouth, more details than he wanted to share poured out. Why couldn't he stop this flood of soul-baring confessions?

"So you up and joined the Army." Camilla skipped over the emotional baggage to focus on his then hoped-for outcome. "Was it just to get away from me?"

"Not entirely. It was to get away from everything."

By joining the Army, he'd set off a bomb in his personal life. His dad had been against it from first mention, and Camilla's attitude toward him now was a direct repercussion of his actions back then. While he had regrets about how he'd handled it, he still stood firm that the decision was the right one. He'd ended things with her in a way that was definitive. If he'd let it drag on, or given her any hope of reconciliation, he'd have only tortured them both and it would have ended up hurting her more in the long run. And clearly, he'd hurt her plenty.

Even now, some days his mood was so dark that several members of staff at his current hospital had worried about his emotional well-being, and had recommended him to administration for counseling. Being forced to confront his own behavior like that had been an experience he could have done without, but it served as proof that he wasn't fit to be in a serious relationship. Reinforced his decision to end their engagement, too.

Camilla gently brought him back to the present conversation. "Your dad was proud of you, even if he didn't agree with your decision to enlist."

"Could've fooled me." A lump rose up in his throat. He pinched the bridge of his nose and tried hard to swallow.

"And now you are a trauma surgeon in Boston?"

The coaxing tone in her voice he remembered well. She'd always been able to pull him away when a conversation grew too intense. Even after everything he'd done to her, she was still looking out for him. Subconsciously, maybe, but she was. Camilla's kind heart and the way she looked after everyone around her was one of the things he had loved about her.

Nodding, he responded to her question. "Emergency attending. I hate the cold, but the pay is good."

The frigid air did a number on his temper, too. The bitterly cold days in the depth of winter were the days his mood was darkest. But he endured the miserable weather because it served a dual purpose for him—first as a penance for the pain he'd caused Camilla and second as a regular reminder that he was far too damaged to maintain a healthy relationship.

"I don't think I could live that far north. I'm a Southern girl at heart."

"I remember when you first moved here. Everyone teased you about your accent. I'm not sure how you moved further south and had a more Southern accent than any of the folks around here."

Camilla rolled her eyes at him. "I didn't sound more Southern, I sounded more country. There's a difference."

"Oh, yeah. And your accent still gets thicker when you're upset, you know." He smiled at the same old argument she'd been presenting for years. The familiar words comforted him, reminding him that they'd had a lot of good times, too. Remembered affection softened his voice on his reply. Her accent had slipped at other times of heightened emotion, too. He'd loved how thick her drawl would get when they'd slipped away during high school and summers during college to spend the evening stargazing out at the lake house.

"Well, you would know. You're the only one who insists on upsetting me every time we end up in the same room."

Danny puffed out a breath slowly. The sentimental moment had passed, too fleeting to hold on to, even if they'd been inclined to do so. For the briefest breath there, he'd allowed himself to consider the what-if, but too much hurt made it impossible. "I'm really not trying to upset you, Camilla. I just want to get on some sort of level ground so that we can move forward here."

"That will be hard when your very existence upsets me," she snapped.

He flinched at the harsh words.

Camilla covered her mouth and her eyes filled with instant regret. "I didn't mean that."

Even if she hadn't meant to snap at him just then, Camilla was not going to make any of this easy on him. That much was clear.

"I think this place is cleaned up enough and we should call it a night before either of us says something else we might regret." He grabbed the broom and took it to the utility closet at the end of the hall. He placed it inside and closed the door. Leaning his head against the cool wood, he tried to soothe the ache her words caused.

"Danny, I'm sorry. I owe you an apology for what I said. Despite all the pain and anger between us, I hope you know that I would never want anything bad to happen to you."

"No?" Being in Greenbriar was going to strip him bare and pull out all those emotions he'd been hiding for so long. "Because it sure sounded heartfelt."

Their eyes met and he wondered what was

going through her mind. What was she think-ing in that moment? He wished he was bet-ter at reading her now. He thought he caught hints of desire, frustration, and maybe even a little fear, but nothing concrete.

The desire was surprising, but he wasn't certain he'd read her right. It was nothing he was confident enough to take a risk on any-way. Things were awkward enough between them without him making an unwanted ad-vance. And given that he had no intentions of starting anything long-term, it was best if he kept his distance. Keeping her at arm's length reduced the chances that he'd hurt her again.

"I'm not sure what came over me. Rest assured, it will not happen again." Camilla smoothed her clothing and her hair.

The alarm on her phone went off.

"Reminder that you have a hot date?"

"Something like that," she murmured.

"Camilla—"

"It will not happen again." He saw the shut-ters slam down in her eyes. "I can trust you to lock up for the night, right? I have some-where I need to be. Will you let the attorney know that I'll stop by and sign whatever he needs signed tomorrow?"

At his nod, she spun on her heels and strode down the hall and out of his sight. He heard the ding of the bell as she went out the front door.

He scrubbed a hand over his face. This was going to be the longest six months of his life.

CHAPTER THREE

WHEN CAMILLA WALKED up to the clinic the next morning after checking on Caden at the hospital, she was surprised to see Danny reclining outside against the worn red brick. With the collar of his coat turned up against the crisp morning air and one foot crossed loosely over the other, he looked deceptively casual, but as someone who'd spent hours admiring his body, she saw through that facade.

His posture stiffened when he caught sight of her and he rose to his full height. The additional inches he had over her and the strength in his broad shoulders had made her feel protected. Butterflies fluttered around in her stomach at the memory of his touch.

"Good morning," she said as she took the key out of her pocket. A hint of pride washed over her when her shaking hands still managed to get the key into the lock on the first try. Letting him see how he still affected her was not on her to-do list for the day, especially after the bomb he'd dropped on her yesterday.

She had spent most of the previous evening trying to look at things from his point of view. She'd been trying to keep his spirits up back then and not let him see her own grief, but had it come across as way too much? In all honesty, it had been one of the hardest times of her life. She'd been terrified that she was going to break down when he'd needed her to be strong. But in hindsight, she had to acknowledge that her over-the-top positivity could well have been suffocating.

"Why didn't you let yourself in?"

"Because I don't actually have keys." Resignation lined his voice and mingled with exhaustion.

"Right."

He'd so thoroughly distracted her that the thought of keys hadn't even crossed her mind. Between their argument and her rush to get to the tutoring session she had every Wednesday evening, she hadn't considered that Danny could need his own set.

Warm air pushed past as she opened the door and they stepped inside out of the winter wind. January and February would be the worst of the wintry weather in Greenbriar.

They didn't get a lot of snow this far south, but frigid air and icy breezes were no strangers to the town.

Camilla unwound her scarf and hung it on the coatrack in the corner of the lobby. "Your dad's keys are probably at the lake house. Did you not see them?"

Danny shook his head and a grimace crossed his face. "I wasn't given the keys to the lake house, either."

She looked him up and down, closely scrutinizing his appearance. An uncharacteristic scruff darkened his normally clean-shaven jaw. Danny still wore the same dark suit he'd had on yesterday, minus the tie, and the rumpled fabric raised a lot more questions in her mind. Had he slept in his clothes last night? Or were the wrinkles from being left on some random woman's floor overnight?

Camilla tried her best to look nonchalant, but her heart ached at the thought of him in someone else's bed. She couldn't stop the question, needing to know the answer. "Where did you stay last night?"

"Why? You worried I found a pretty little shoulder to cry on?" The defensive tone contradicted the slight affront he tried to hide.

Interesting. So he was insulted that she thought he'd stayed with another woman.

She wasn't sure if she should address it and confront the issue outright, or just let it go with the resolution to keep her distance from Danny Owens. It wasn't any of her business if he'd found someone to spend the night with. What did she care who he chose to spend his time with?

Yet she couldn't help but feel relieved that he'd been alone last night. They hadn't been a couple in years, so whose bed he slept in shouldn't matter to her, but it so did and that spark of jealousy frustrated her. She tried to pivot from accusation to concern, desperate to cover up her interest in his personal life. "I was actually worried you might have slept in your car, if you must know."

Before she could say anything else, Danny changed the subject. "So, before we got, uh... derailed last night, I'd brought up selling you my share of this clinic."

He sat on the edge of the front desk, managing to look both perfectly at home and completely out of place at the same time. Reconciling the man in front of her with the man she'd loved and lost might take some time. There was a different energy about him, a somberness to his gaze that held secrets. Secrets that she shouldn't want to expose to the light of day, and she shouldn't want to soothe those fine worry lines around his eyes, either.

Stop it, Camilla. He's off-limits.

"Were you serious?"

Knowing she shouldn't look a gift horse in the mouth, she still couldn't stop the question that slipped past her lips. If he sold her his half of the clinic, it would be hers exclusively. She could put her name in large letters on that front window and make all the decisions. It would check the box on one of her biggest dreams—to own her own medical practice.

"Yes, I'm one hundred percent serious about that. I admit last night I second-guessed it a bit, worried that I'd be dishonoring my father's memory or letting him down somehow. But you were right. This is your clinic, and other than my last name on the plaque, I have no claim here. You've put in the sweat equity and my father should have recognized that. We'll get the attorney to draw up the paperwork for you to buy me out when the time comes, if that's what you want, or we can sell it outright if you'd prefer."

"Just like that?" She searched his gaze, watching every micro-expression on his face. After his outburst at the will reading, something about Danny giving in this easily felt off. The Danny she'd known never backed down, so she'd geared up for battle on this, because she wasn't giving up her clinic without a fight. And having him step aside so reasonably just sanded the grit right off her.

Shrugging, he agreed, "Just like that. I figured we could spend some time fixing the place up—it will help it sell if you don't want to buy me out. We can alternate days working, or you can see the patients and I'll do the renovating. Minimize how much time we spend together whenever we can. I'd like to get out of this and back to my life with as little drama as possible."

And there was the angle she'd been looking for. She knew there had to be one.

"Get out of this…"

Of course, once again, Danny just wanted to run away from Greenbriar. Away from her… He didn't want to be tied down to this sleepy little community. That couldn't be plainer if he'd painted it on the water tower in hot pink spray paint like the love note he'd put there in their senior year of high school.

As a member of the town council, his father had been furious about the three-foot-high letters telling everyone in Greenbriar that Danny loved Camilla. As a seventeen-year-old girl, though, it had been the most romantic thing anyone had ever done for her.

It still was, if she was being honest.

Seeing him profess his love to the entire town like that had made things real for her. She'd naively thought Danny treasured her love like she'd treasured his; after all his painted words had proved it. Eagerly, she'd shown him that night how much his actions had meant to her. The paint proved more durable than their love, however, so while the now faded pink words still graced the side of the water tower, they no longer served as a romantic memento, but were a haunting reminder of heartbreak and love lost.

But words were just words, and they meant nothing if the person writing them wasn't sincere. Maybe he had been earnest in that moment, maybe he had loved her in some small way once upon a time, but his feelings had faded like the paint on the tower. She hadn't been able to give him what he needed.

No matter what she did, it never seemed enough. Her own parents had chosen drugs over her. She hadn't been able to keep a foster family. Or a fiancé... So many tears had been shed over people who'd probably never blinked an eye at never being near her again.

She looked away from Danny. Picking up the crispy brown fern behind the reception desk, she sighed. She must have forgotten to water the poor thing while trying to keep everyone in Greenbriar healthy and help Robert through his last days. She hugged it to her chest. Even plants refused to stick with her and chose to die instead.

She was never enough.

"Are you even listening to me?" Danny interrupted her thoughts as he stood up, came around the desk and invaded her personal space.

"Hmm." She jerked herself back to the present. There'd be time enough for self-pity when she was home alone with her dog. At least Fidget loved her unconditionally.

His brow wrinkled in concern. "Are you okay?"

Taking a step away from Danny, she answered his question. "Yes, I definitely want to buy you out. What are your terms?" Camilla blinked rapidly, trying to keep any tears from falling and ruining her mascara. She was stronger than this. She didn't cry over decade-old memories or dead plants.

Danny laid a hand on her shoulder, the weight comforting and confusing all at once. "Can I get you anything? Water? What do you want?"

She wanted to chastise him for wanting to run away again. She wanted to curse him for all the pain he'd caused her. She wanted to kiss him until he remembered how good they were together. Love him so deeply that he'd fall in love with her all over again, because the pain she still felt at his presence said she wasn't completely over him.

But life didn't work that way.

And she certainly wasn't telling him all that and exposing herself to further rejection. If she'd learned anything, it was that she couldn't trust Danny Owens with her heart.

"I just realized this plant is beyond help. I'm going to go dispose of it before our first patient arrives." She lifted the plant slightly to emphasize her words and hopefully draw his attention from her face long enough to pull herself together.

Danny's head tilted as he considered her answer, but he thankfully didn't call her on it. "You don't happen to know if my dad kept a spare key to the lake house anywhere here, do you? I'd really like to shower and change before the service."

Fumbling a little, she managed to get the key to the lake house off her key ring without upending the lifeless fern onto the carpet. Wordlessly, she handed it to him.

"Thanks. I'll see you at the funeral?"

Camilla nodded, not trusting herself to

speak. Her emotions were getting the best of her in that moment. While she could control them if she stayed quiet, she wasn't sure she could say the same if she opened her mouth. Words might come out, or equally it could be sobs.

He strode out the door, the little bell chiming his departure gaily. And she sank down, her back against the wall, still cradling the lamented maidenhair.

"It's going to be a long six months," she said aloud. Looking up at the anniversary portrait of her late boss and his wife, she shook her head. "I don't know why you thought this was a good idea, Robert. Danny has made his position crystal clear, and no amount of wishing is going to change the course he's charted."

She drew in a deep breath. When she'd woken up that morning, she'd known she would have to face Danny again at the funeral, but he'd caught her unaware by showing up at the clinic before opening. That had thrown off her entire game plan for dealing with him. She'd expected to have the buffer of a crowd to soften the interactions between them.

She couldn't let him close enough to upend her foundation this time. The fact that she'd never seen their breakup coming had rocked her axis entirely. Usually a dying relationship showed some signs of withering first—unanswered calls, secrets, or lies, but theirs hadn't. At least, not anything visible to her. So when he'd ended things so swiftly, she'd been gobsmacked. Looking back now, she could see some of the cracks in their relationship; she could see how he had shut down and needed a different tactic from her, but the fact remained that he'd broken up with her without so much as a discussion. With how she'd prided herself on reading people, it had really shaken her confidence.

What was that old saying? Pride goeth before a fall?

Yeah. She'd certainly fallen. Danny's rejection had been a massive hit to her pride, but she wouldn't let him catch her off guard again. They'd get through Robert's funeral today and they'd meet to discuss a schedule for how to manage things at the clinic with minimal interaction. That was a discussion she was prepared for. After that, she saw no reason why they even had to be in the same room at the same time.

It was safer for her heart if she put some distance back between them.

The bell over the door chimed as her first patient of the day came through. She rose swiftly to greet them, tossing the dead plant into the trash can.

If only the memories of a lost love were so easily banished.

The funeral home had been bursting at the seams as everyone in Greenbriar came to pay their respects to his father—a cherished member of their community. With barely space to breathe, claustrophobia sent his heart racing and the dark edges of a panic attack were banging at his crumbling defenses long before the service was over. The only thing that had kept him from crossing over that fine line between okay and not was the soft hand Camilla had slipped into his when the pastor began to speak. He wasn't sure if she took his hand to comfort him or because she needed comfort herself, but he'd desperately needed that connection. Her touch kept him grounded until his father's casket was carried out to the waiting hearse. He'd followed closely behind and sucked in a deep breath as he stood next to the provided family car. The cold invaded his lungs and made his chest ache, but it staved off the emotional breakdown.

The processional made the slow trek from downtown Greenbriar out to the cemetery on the outskirts of town. Danny made the ride alone, having no other family to join him in the limousine. Camilla had declined to go with him, insisting on driving her own car. Only minimal road noise interrupted the quiet within the vehicle. Danny wasn't sure the silence was any better than the bustle of the crowded funeral home. It gave him far too much space to think before the long, black car drew to a stop near where his mother and brother had been buried and where his father was about to join them.

Icy air whistled through the trees and yet a crowd of black-clad people soon stood next to the open grave. Despite the bitter cold, the sun shone brilliantly across the headstones all around them. The day should have been damp and gray: it would have been more fitting for a day of mourning.

His father had arranged every detail. All Danny had needed to do was show up. From the music played at the funeral home to the hymn they'd just finished singing here at the graveside, his father had preplanned everything. Danny frowned; he should have had to do something, plan something. Wasn't that part of grieving for a lost loved one? The final decisions made for their remembrance?

"Dr. Robert Owens was one of the very best men I've known, and I know a lot of people," Reverend Fitch said, his breath coming in visible puffs. A few people snickered at his little joke, but it was true. The man had presided over his mother's and brother's funerals, as well as marrying most of Danny's classmates—at least the ones who'd stayed in Greenbriar. "A loving husband and devoted father, Robert was a real role model to the younger generations here in our town. While we hate to say goodbye to him, we know that he's now reunited in heaven with his beloved wife, Linda, and their treasured youngest son, Robby. Let us bow our heads in a final farewell."

All around, heads bowed. The only noise was the occasional ruffle of someone turning up a collar or the wind itself. Silence dwelled as an entire town bid adieu to one of their favorite people.

Slowly, one by one, heads rose and people came up to Danny, offering their condolences for his loss. Each mourner shared stories of how his father had saved their life, or provided financial support when they'd lost a job or a family member, or some other unforgettable act of kindness.

He'd known his father had held a prominent place in Greenbriar. That hadn't been a surprise, but he hadn't realized quite how many lives his father had touched so deeply. These people stood out in frigid weather to say goodbye, and their faces were lined with genuine grief. Like him, they were saying goodbye to someone they loved.

Glancing over at Camilla, he saw that she was also receiving stories and condolences. But unlike the deferential way they spoke to him, they spoke to her like she was family. He got respectful handshakes and an occasional pat on the arm, while Camilla was swept into hugs and lingering embraces.

Hmm.

She'd cemented her place in the local society in a way that he—despite being Greenbriar born and bred—hadn't accomplished. Like his father, she was beloved by these people. They would grieve for her if she was gone, like they grieved now for his father.

Who would miss me?

The thought cut through him harsher than the wind whipping past the gravestones and he inhaled sharply, trying once again to bring oxygen into his suddenly suffocating lungs. As the last of the well-wishers made their way back to their warm cars and out of the cemetery, Danny couldn't help wondering if he'd have more than a handful of colleagues show up at his funeral. He had friends, of course, from his Army days, but they were scattered across the country. Now he had a few friendly coworkers whom he spent very little time with outside work.

Would anyone grieve for him?

He stood watching as they lowered his father's casket into the ground next to his mother's. With both of his parents and his only brother gone, he had no family left. The mother who'd held him tight and kissed his boo-boos, the brother he'd fought with and fought for over the years, both taken in a single moment. And now, the father who'd taught him what it meant to stand up straight and the importance of keeping your word, taken from him without the chance to say goodbye to him, either.

Kicking at a loose clod of dirt, he sank further into the turmoil these thoughts created in his mind. The guilt that had forced his hand in pushing away Camilla had also driven him straight to the recruiter's office. Instead of taking one of the fellowships he'd been offered, Danny had joined the Army to get away from Greenbriar.

He'd skipped over any risks in favor of the adrenaline rush that came with being a trauma surgeon. But somewhere along the way, the Army had become more to him. It had given him a purpose. It had become a deeper calling, that desire to serve his country. What had been initially a penance for his failures to save his mom and brother had become his salvation, too. But his Army career had kept him on a lonely path.

Swallowing hard, he realized that he had no community, and he couldn't think of a single person who would be truly upset that they didn't get to say goodbye if he was gone.

But being alone was what he'd signed up for, wasn't it?

He'd chosen to be alone when he'd ended things with Camilla. He was toxic to those who got close to him, so he pushed them away. He couldn't be trusted with loved ones; they always ended up hurt because of him. That knowledge had kept him from letting anyone else get too close. He dated, sure, but whenever things started to become even slightly serious, he always walked away.

Look where that had gotten him—standing alone at his father's grave with no shoulder to cry on. No loved ones to go home with or turn to in the middle of the night when the grief became too much to bear alone. He'd kept everyone at arm's length and now he had to face up to the reality of that.

There was a quiver in his breath as he

watched the shovels full of dirt cascade down almost in slow motion, marring the polished wood surface of the casket. With each layer of soil, his heart ached more and more as the finality of the situation really dug in. The last person in his life who loved him was now six feet under. He'd never felt more isolated than he did in that moment.

"Do you want me to send the car back? I can wait for you." Camilla stood next to him, watching as the dirt poured down over the no longer visible casket. "It's okay to cry, you know."

He sniffed. Cry? Here? No. His tears would only come when there would be no witnesses in case he became a blubbering baboon. "Was there anyone in town not here today?"

She let out a soft snort. "I don't think so. They even closed the diner."

"Have you ever wondered exactly who'd miss you if you died?" He looked over at her and then shook his head. Everyone in town loved her; of course she didn't worry about something like that. "Never mind. I saw how the people flocked to you today. You've really grown into your own here and they'd be lost without you."

She smiled at him. "I do know what that feels like, though. Until you came into my life, I knew that no one would miss me, and that was a fact, not a silly worry. For what it's worth, though, Danny, I'd miss you."

He rolled her words around in his mind, trying to decipher the truth. She hated him, didn't she? After all the pain he'd caused her, how could she claim that she'd miss him?

"Sure." He scoffed, unable to reconcile her statement with her recent actions. "You've spent the better half of the last two days yelling at me."

"Maybe I like having someone to argue with?" Her tone held a teasing note.

Danny reached for Camilla's hand. Her soft skin was warm despite the chill in the air. Their fingers intertwined like they'd done a billion times in the past. A new tension between them kept the simple gesture from feeling familiar, though.

"You've always been my favorite person to argue with," he said, tugging her closer, not wanting to let the connection between them lapse.

Camilla's lips parted and he caught the flash of pink as her tongue darted out to moisten her lips. His head bent toward hers, their mouths only a breath apart. Kissing Camilla would be an epically bad decision, but he wasn't sure he had the strength to stop himself from making it.

"Making up after a fight has never been so fun as when I was making up with you."

Camilla stiffened at his words. "This is a bad idea. We've had far more than a fight. Danny. We've practically fought an emotional war. I can't…" Without another word, she spun and walked to her car. He recognized the angry set of her shoulders.

Maybe he'd taken the flirting a bit too far, since he didn't plan on following through with anything. It wouldn't be fair to her if he started something he had no intention of finishing. He wanted to put Greenbriar in his rearview as soon as the terms of the will had been fulfilled, didn't he?

But what he wanted most of all in that moment was to find a way to banish that deep-seated sense of being completely and utterly alone in the world.

And he had no idea where to start.

CHAPTER FOUR

"COME ON, FIDGET," Camilla said, trying desperately to distract her dog from the French fries someone had dropped on the sidewalk and left there. "Those are yucky. We don't eat yucky things."

But the little black-and-white mutt she'd adopted last summer most certainly did eat yucky things she found on the street. In fact, the yuckier the better in Fidget's opinion. Looking rather like a dirty mop, the shih tzu mix pranced along beside her with the French fry dangling from her mouth that she'd managed to snag before Camilla could pull her away.

"Oh, Camilla, dear!"

Camilla closed her eyes briefly before turning around with a forced smile plastered on her face. It was barely above freezing this morning and yet this was the third person to stop her for a chat. Was a peaceful walk with her dog really too much to ask for?

Apparently so.

"Hello, Mrs. Sutherland. How are you this morning?" Camilla glanced down the street toward her house. So close, yet it might as well be miles.

Wrapping her bright pink robe more tightly around herself against the early morning temperatures, Mrs. Sutherland pursed her lips and said, "My gout is acting up, but that's not why I stopped you."

Camilla had never thought the woman had interrupted her walk for a medical reason. Mrs. Sutherland was far too much of a gossip for that. A quick glance at her watch showed that she had just over a half hour to get the dog home, settle her down for the day, and make it to work.

"Oh?" she asked, despite being absolutely certain that she knew what her elderly neighbor wanted to talk about. She tried to keep her tone conversational, but not too eager. Mrs. Sutherland could gossip for hours if she had a willing audience, but the elderly woman was also the first to call with a casserole if someone was ailing and she never failed to toss in a few bills whenever she saw a collection being taken for a family in need, despite her own fixed income.

"I wanted to know if Danny Owens was coming back to town." The rolled newspaper in her hand was waved around like a conductor might wave his baton while directing a symphony. The faded pink rollers in her hair bobbed along with every movement. "If anyone here knows, it would be you. Don't think I didn't know about the two of you sneaking into my shed together doing Lord knows what. Why, the two of you used to be thick as thieves! But I suppose that changed after... Well, it was a horrible thing, the way that boy just tap-danced across your heart like it was a slab of hardwood and skulked out of town like a thief in the night. Watching you put yourself back together after all that took so much strength. Have I ever told you how proud I am of you for doing that?"

Camilla shook her head.

"Well, I am. We all are. You were Robert's rock through it all. He'd never have made it as long as he did without you. Anyhow, what news comes from over that way?"

"All I know is that Danny is supposed to be here for the next six months." Camilla pressed her lips together tightly and held in the rest of what she wanted to say. Since Robert's funeral, it seemed as though every person in town had dredged up memories of Danny, when she'd rather those painful remnants stayed buried in the muck and mire with the rest of her past.

Mrs. Sutherland leaned in and fake-whispered, "I heard rumors... Well, you probably don't care to hear them. And you know how rumors go."

Rumors had been swirling since the funeral. Camilla tried really hard not to listen to what everyone was saying, especially when it involved her, but at the same time, she couldn't help being curious. Danny was her partner in the clinic now, after all. She had a need to know what was going on in his life, or so she told herself. And since their six months of working together at the clinic to satisfy the terms of the will officially started that day, she was having trouble getting Danny off her mind.

Had he returned to town? She certainly hadn't laid eyes on him since the day of the funeral. He'd left her a voice mail at the office saying he had to get back to Boston and they would discuss the practice when he returned, but nothing since. What if he left her hanging and she lost all that she had been working for?

After realizing that she'd stopped listening to Mrs. Sutherland's rambles and was quite possibly being rude to the older woman, Camilla wrapped up the conversation quickly. "I'm so sorry, ma'am, but I need to get Fidget here home so that I can get to work. I have patients soon."

Four houses down from Mrs. Sutherland, Camilla headed up the driveway to the large four-square she'd inherited. The pale green house had a stately beauty to it, with a wide porch spanning the front, and the currently empty window boxes that she'd fill with colorful flowers in the warmer months to come. As she unlocked the front door, she ran her fingers across the little brass numbers she'd put on the door herself and sent up a little thank-you to the man who'd left her the first home she'd ever truly known.

It was within these very walls that she'd learned what a true family could look like. Her heart and soul had been filled with love and acceptance under this roof. Robert had recognized that and chosen to honor her with the ownership of this house, surely knowing that it would be her forever home. She finally had the roots she'd been trying to grow for years.

Sadly, she had no one to share it with but

a shaggy little stray prone to scavenging for scraps. Longing for companionship, she'd adopted the dog to stave off some of the loneliness. While it did help, nothing would really fill that particular void but a human family. Someday, Camilla promised herself, these walls would be filled with the love and laughter of a family again—her family. She picked Fidget up and gave the little dog a cuddle that was more for her own benefit than the dog's.

Fidget fussed about being put in her crate, but after getting a massive vet bill because the dog had eaten things she shouldn't and after nearly losing her, Camilla didn't fall for the tucked-tail routine anymore. "Quit pouting. You know it isn't going to work. The crate is for your safety, after all. Bye, Fidget. I'll see you at lunch, okay?"

Camilla checked the weather on her cell phone before making the decision to walk to work. Clear and cold, the app said. No inclement weather expected. So she set out on foot. It was only two and a half blocks from her front door to the clinic, and she hated to parallel park if she could at all avoid it.

What would she do if Danny didn't come back? Leaving Greenbriar wasn't an option, and the terms of the will wouldn't allow her to buy the building or the practice directly if Danny flaked on her. At the end of Baker Street, she paused. There was an old hardware store that had closed up last year when the owner retired and moved to Atlanta to be near his grandchildren. It had sat empty for months now. It was the only commercial property she knew of for sale in Greenbriar, and it would take a ton of effort to convert it to a medical clinic, but it might be her only option if push came to shove.

With a sigh, she continued her trek to the clinic. No use borrowing trouble and worrying about things that had yet to come. She'd see patients in her living room if she had to. She was a doctor, and a darn good one. She'd briefly thought about doing a surgical residency, and she'd done a rotation in the emergency room where the fast pace had nearly convinced her that specialty wasn't for her. Her heart, though, was truly in being a general practitioner. She loved developing that relationship with her young patients and watching them grow. Making elders' final years more comfortable was heartwarming, even as she knew her time with them drew to a close. She truly enjoyed seeing people of all stages in life and she loved spending the time with them that was needed to really get to the root of their troubles.

"Did I see you looking at the old hardware store?"

She looked over to see Danny pulling something—was that a wallpaper steamer?—from the bed of a pickup truck with Massachusetts license plates.

"Just looking at my options."

"You didn't think I was coming back, did you?" He raised a single eyebrow and that simple action took her heart on a jog.

Why did her stupid, traitorous body insist on reacting to his every move? Even if she could recall exactly how amazing his hands had felt on her skin and how loved she'd felt when wrapped in his embrace. *Remember how it felt when he took his ring back?* That thought put her back into the right mindset to deal with Danny. It killed the little hint of interest that his silly eyebrow had sparked. It was just an eyebrow, for goodness' sake! What would she do if he flashed her some abs—strip like an exotic dancer?

When she replied to his question, the ice in her tone surprised even her. "Well, it wouldn't be the first time that you'd put Greenbriar in your rearview without a second glance."

Or me.

Silence hung between them thick with accusation. Danny's eyes glittered with anger, but Camilla refused to be cowed by it. Although she hadn't quite meant to be so cold, the sentiment behind her words held true.

Honestly, her pride wouldn't let her back down from this fight. She was a young, healthy, more than reasonably attractive woman—if she did say so herself—and she was no longer going to allow this man to make her feel badly about herself. She'd spent years questioning her self-worth both before and after Danny Owens had made his mark on her life. Only in the last few had she finally found a modicum of confidence and she refused to let him destroy it.

"Fair enough," he grumbled, dropping his gaze.

With his concession, Camilla opened the door and let them into the clinic. She took down the after-hours sign. Her hands shook as she tucked the sign into the drawer on the table by the door and hoped Danny didn't see what standing up to him had cost her.

Putting on a brave front, and standing up for herself, was self-preservation—a skill she'd learned early in life. But it never got easier. No matter how many times she had to do it, her nerves grew raw each time.

"Since the people here are probably more comfortable with you, I thought I'd let you see patients while I worked on bringing this place into the current century." He tapped on the wallpaper and said, "Starting with this lobby. I'll do one side at a time so that the patients won't be subjected to a construction zone."

"You decided this all on your own, did you?"

She crossed her arms over her chest. How dare he think he could just show up and make changes to her medical practice? Okay, half hers, but he had no interest in lingering in Greenbriar and running this practice. He'd said as much. And somehow that translated in his thick skull as "change whatever you like."

No. Absolutely not.

"Did you think that maybe this was a decision you should have run past me first as your *partner*?"

His lips tightened in silent acknowledgement of the truth in her question. "I was going to let you pick the paint or whatever after this. But this—" he waved a hand at the wallpaper "—has to go."

Temper settling slightly, she moved her head up and down in agreement. She'd hated that wallpaper at first sight and it wasn't one of those things that grew on you with time.

"That doesn't mean you make these decisions without me, even if you think for sure I will agree." A huff of frustration rushed over her lips. "I'm the one planning to stay here, Danny. If either of us should make decisions about the decor, it should be me."

He nodded solemnly and then his face softened into a smile. "All right, I'll paint it all teal. That's still your favorite color, isn't it?"

He'd remembered her favorite color after all these years? She swallowed hard at the lump in her throat. That once upon a time he had cared enough to learn things about her stabbed down to her very soul. She wasn't prepared for a reminder of when things had been good.

"I think a neutral would be better," she finally choked out before hurrying down the hallway to her office. She slammed the door and leaned against the cold wood, desperately fighting for a scrap of composure.

One hundred and eighty days to go. One hundred and eighty days of trying to stop her galloping heart from racing out of her chest every time Danny flashed her that crooked grin.

One hundred and eighty days of desperately trying to forget how the man she'd loved had thrown her away like a crumpled newspaper while not falling for him again or ruining all her plans for the future.

* * *

"What did I say?"

Danny watched as Camilla strode down the hall, knowing he'd upset her, but not entirely sure how. He ran the conversation through his head over and over. Line by line he analyzed his words and her reactions. She seemed most upset about him remembering her favorite color. How was that bad?

Women, he shook his head. He'd never understand them. Really, wouldn't it have been worse if he had forgotten how much she loved any shade of teal, from the palest of hues to the deep dark, almost black shades?

His Camilla would have loved the fact he'd remembered her favorite color. This version was nothing like the woman he'd loved. He hadn't had much time to really consider all the changes in Camilla while packing up his life in Boston and moving back to Greenbriar.

Or are you just too worried about what you might discover when you do think about it?

This Camilla had a softness to her that the old version had lacked. She'd embraced a new style, her clothing now classic but feminine. Her long hair she left down in soft waves, or pulled back in a clip when she was with a patient, rather than twisted up tight in a bun or a ponytail. The tomboy in secondhand duds he'd first fallen for was nowhere to be found, and in her place stood a strong, beautiful woman with scars on her soul. A core strength now emanated from her, one that he envied. She'd done a far better job putting herself back together than he had.

Even in the familiarity of her touch, there was a difference, a newness that intrigued him. She'd been the best friend he'd ever had, his first—and only—real love. After the accident where his mom and brother died, and he'd been laid up in the hospital, she had barely left his side. The idea that she wouldn't have been strong enough to handle his mental struggles he could see now was a fragile construct that wouldn't hold up to too much scrutiny.

But if that linchpin of all his decisions regarding their relationship wasn't solid, then what else had he lied to himself about?

Those thoughts were entirely too much to unpack in that moment. Truth be told, he wasn't ready for the emotional maelstrom they'd bring into his life.

Turning his attention outside those difficult thoughts to the outdated lobby, he decided where to start. He began by rearranging some of the chairs, moving more to the side with the reception desk and clearing out space around the opposite wall. By starting on that side, he wouldn't have to move the computer or the file cabinets yet.

He eyed the old metal file cabinets. A fresh coat of paint on them wouldn't hide the dents and dings of age. He wondered if Camilla would be open to digitizing all the files so they could get rid of those ancient things. His dad would have clung to his beloved paper records as if they were his lifeline in an ocean of lost information, but Camilla had surely worked with digital records and computerized patient information in med school and residency. He'd save that subject for a day when she didn't look like she wanted to rip his head off and use it as a bowling ball.

After filling the wallpaper steamer with water in the small kitchen, he moved back to the reception area. Deciding it best to start at the door and work his way around the room, he plugged the steamer up to heat. Before he got to work, though, he gave in to his nagging sense of wrongdoing and went to apologize to Camilla for upsetting her.

He was going to have to guard his words and maybe hold some things back to make it through the next several months with minimal drama. Camilla deserved that much consideration after what he'd put her through, so even though he still wasn't sure what he had done, he knew he had to concede that something had gone wrong and it was clearly his fault. Tapping lightly on her office door, he waited for her acknowledgment before opening it. "Hey, I am going to get started on getting this wallpaper off, but before I do, I wanted to apologize. I realize I upset you, and I'm sorry for that."

Camilla crossed her arms over her chest and stared at him. Anger glittered in her eyes. She gave off the distinct impression that she didn't believe a word he was saying.

He took a steadying breath and tried again. "I mean that, Camilla. The last thing I want to do is hurt you more, although this likely won't be the last time I upset you given that we will be in close proximity until August."

"I'm putting in a supply order today. I have the list on my desk if you want to glance over it and make any additions."

He recognized the tactic. Camilla always changed the subject when the conversation got too personal for her to keep a tight rein on her emotions. Hopefully, that meant she was taking his apology to heart. Danny scuffed his foot across the carpet, staring at the slight color change as he shifted the pile with his sole. The carpet in this office could stand to be replaced, too, he thought idly.

"So, are we good?" he asked.

"I suppose we are until the next time you decide to make decisions without me," she snapped. "From office decor to marriage, you seem to think me incapable of making rational choices."

Closing his eyes, Danny leaned against the doorframe. Before he left Greenbriar, he'd have to address their past, but it couldn't be today. The mental fortitude required to do this discussion justice was just out of reach for him today.

"It was me. It was all me. You shouldn't take any of it personally." Anger at himself for making her feel so inadequate rose up sharp and fast. She was a beautiful, successful doctor who shouldn't be made to feel less than that for anyone, certainly not a broken man too stupid to see her strength. He was scum for putting her in that position.

"How could I not?" Camilla scoffed. "You told me—word for word—*I wasn't enough*. That I would *never* be enough. It took me years to work through the damage your rejection did to my self-worth. I blamed myself for so long, wondering what I'd done wrong, what I could have done differently that might have changed your mind about us. Worrying that there'd been another woman, that it was because of my background. To know that you moved on, when I never really could..." She broke off with what sounded suspiciously like a sob. Eyes closed, she took a deep breath, and when she opened them, the cold fury in her eyes sent a shiver down his spine. "But I guess I learned what I'd always really known, that men can't ever be trusted."

"I'm an idiot. It's the best explanation I've got right now." He pushed himself upright. The depth of the wounds he'd dealt her were far worse than he'd thought, but the full truth might hurt her even more and he wasn't ready to divulge just how messed up he had been. Still was, if he was being honest with himself. "I think maybe we should just leave the past in the past where it belongs, don't you?"

"Fine."

"I'm going to work on that wallpaper now."

"We need to have a plan in place for what we are going to do after you get the wallpaper off. You can't just jump right in and have my medical practice look like a work in progress."

"Fine. I'll take my wallpaper steamer and go home for the day. You can work in *our* practice while I relax on the dock."

As he slowly moved back to the front of the building, he thought he heard Camilla call him a coward. She was right—he was a coward. At least when it came to her and the mistakes he'd made with her.

At the time he'd broken off their engagement, Danny had been convinced that she was better off without him in her life. He'd justified that decision with the belief that she'd move on quickly, like the stories she'd told him of moving from foster family to foster family with no permanent attachments. He'd told himself that her love for him wasn't permanent. It would fade with time and she would find someone else, someone more worthy of her. But the pain in her eyes just now made him realize a hard truth about himself—all his rationalizations were built on falsehoods and weren't worth a dime. All of them, not just the notion that she wasn't strong enough to withstand the darkness within his soul.

His breath was ragged as he picked up the wallpaper steamer. What else had he deluded himself about?

CHAPTER FIVE

TGIF. Camilla sighed. Awkward didn't cover how their first month of working in the same office felt. The days had passed at an agonizing pace—slower than a turtle. They'd both tiptoed around the other, somehow avoiding any further arguments or hurt feelings, but the tension of working side by side for four weeks was taking its toll.

She sank into the chair at the reception desk and looked around at the bare walls, splotchy white mud patches against the aged gray of the drywall. Her three o'clock patient had called to reschedule and she found herself with a little downtime alone while Danny ran to the next town to pick up paint for the lobby. He was planning to paint this weekend when there wouldn't be patients trekking through the office and potentially through the wet paint. It was one of the few things they'd agreed on finally. It had taken them well over a week just to agree on a paint color and when it would be best to start on the wallpaper removal.

Leaning back, Camilla closed her eyes and tried to push all the conflict and concerns out of her mind. In less than an hour, the foster teen she was caring for over the weekend would be dropped off and she wanted to get herself completely together.

She had done respite care before, but had needed to stop when Robert had gotten so ill. Given her past, she wished she could do more, but her job wouldn't allow her to foster full-time or adopt at the moment. But with Danny here now, he could be on call since he planned to be at the clinic to paint anyways. And that left her free to play a small part in helping some foster parents have a break, and allowed her to show a teen that someone indeed cared and that being in the foster system didn't guarantee a bleak outlook. She regularly went as a mentor to the group home where she'd spent her final two years of foster care. It was one of her tutoring kids who was spending the weekend with her, in fact. Her hopes were that she could serve as a role model. If she could touch just one life positively, the effort would be worth it.

The tiny bell over the door jingled and Camilla straightened up, forcing a smile to her face that she hoped didn't look too fake.

"Dr. D., guess who got a B+ on that science test you helped her study for?"

"The same girl who is referring to herself in third person?" Camilla's pleasure now was genuine as she smiled indulgently at Maddie, the fourteen-year-old she'd been tutoring through freshman biology.

The teen's face lit up and she laughed like Camilla's words were the funniest thing she'd ever heard. "Good one, Dr. D. And yeah, you're right. It is me, the one and only Maddie B with a B+ in bio!"

"I'm so proud of you! I knew you could do it. High five!"

Maddie came over and slapped her hand against Camilla's before she hopped up to sit cross-legged on the reception desk. "Mrs. Stone said she'll be here in a few for you to sign off on the paperwork for watching me this weekend. She's picking up a couple last-minute things before they go out of town."

"That's fine. I have one more patient scheduled for today and then we'll go back to my place. What sounds better—movie night or game night? Either way, I have popcorn and ice cream."

"Both?"

Laughter filled the reception area and covered up the tinkling of the bell over the door.

"Dang, Dr. D. Who is *that*?" Maddie grabbed a flyer for the state children's health insurance program and fanned herself with it, faking a swoon. "That your man?"

Camilla looked over to see Danny, his muscular arms laden with painting supplies. "That guy? Nah… That's Dr. Owens."

"Oh, I gotcha. He's the new partner you were telling me about." Maddie eyed Danny with an eagerness far too adult for her age. A heaviness settled over Camilla at the realization of all Maddie must have experienced. She'd have to have a talk with the young girl about men and sex, for sure.

Danny looked uncomfortable at being the subject of the girl's scrutiny. He set the paint supplies off in the corner before turning to face them. "Sorry to interrupt."

Maddie hopped off the desk and sashayed over to him, offering her hand. "I'm Maddie."

"Dr. Owens," Danny said, not offering his first name. He gave Maddie's hand a very brief shake and then put more distance between them.

He moved over to the reception desk and leaned on the wall near where Camilla sat. "I picked up all the paint and supplies. Figured

I'd get started tonight. Was gonna ask if you wanted to help me, but I see you are otherwise occupied."

"I don't mind helping," Maddie offered. Her words had a flirty tone that set up an awkward mood. Although far too young to be hitting on a grown man, Maddie seemed unaware of the impropriety. "Whatever you need."

"We already have plans for a *girls-only* movie and game night, remember?" Camilla shut the idea down. She trusted *Danny* to not cross that line, but Maddie was a different story. Camilla had been in Maddie's shoes and she knew how appealing an adult male with a job could look, and when that man looked like Danny, well, it was just best for them all to keep a little distance between them.

"Sorry I'm running late," Alma Stone called out as she walked through the door, her three-year-old son trailing behind her. "I swear, time has just gotten away from me today. We are leaving for Dave's sister's wedding in less than an hour and I still need to put gas in the car and drop Bennie off to the sitter. I still don't understand why they had to have a fancy wedding that we couldn't bring the kids to, but it's my sister-in-law, so I can hardly skip it."

She stopped short. "Danny Owens? Is that you?"

"Hey, uh, Alma." Danny sounded uncertain about the name of their former classmate, but thankfully he'd gotten it right. Alma was touchy about being confused with her twin sister, Amy. "How have you been?"

"I was so sorry to hear about your dad. Such a fine man and gone too young. I hated to miss the service, but Bennie was running a temp. Just a little sniffle, thankfully, but I didn't want to take him out in that cold air and expose everyone in case it was more."

"It's fine, Alma." Danny offered a reassurance to the chattering woman.

"Well, thank you for saying that. You were always so kind. All us girls were so jealous when Camilla here was the one to win your affections—oh, shoot. I didn't mean to bring up bad memories." Alma winced.

In high school, Alma had been the girl who never stopped talking. That hadn't changed. Fortunately, she'd grown a bit of an awareness to the pain her chatterbox ways caused others. Sadly, sometimes only after the words had slipped through her open lips.

"We have had our issues in the past, of

course, but we are in a good place now. Aren't we, Danny?" Camilla said lightly.

"Better than we've been in years," he said with an earnestness that couldn't be denied.

Camilla stood. She wanted to get Alma out of the office before her old classmate brought up more history that Camilla would rather Maddie not hear. She wanted to set a good example for Maddie and her own past had been a little rocky at times. "Do you have those papers for me, Alma? I have a patient due any second and you did say you were in a hurry, right?"

The other woman looked a little flustered but pulled some folded paperwork out of her purse. "And you are good with dropping Maddie at school on Monday? We are going to be in sometime real late on Sunday night and I wouldn't want to wake either of you up."

"I will drop her off at the front steps myself and make sure she walks in before I drive away," Camilla assured Alma. They'd had their differences, mostly due to Alma's constant blabbering, but Alma really was a dedicated foster mother who truly tried to make Maddie and the other kids she'd had over the years feel wanted and at home.

Alma took the signed papers from Camilla and stuffed them back into her purse. "Okay,

Maddie, you be good while we are gone. Listen to Dr. Devereaux. I'll text you and check in, but you feel free to call or text me anytime you want, okay, sweetie?"

"Yes, ma'am." Maddie nodded dutifully.

Alma gave the girl a brief hug, which was still more touch than Maddie seemed to want from her foster mother. Camilla had shied away from physical touch for a large part of her life, feeling unwanted or unloved, too. It made her more determined to help Maddie see that she had people in her corner.

"Thank God she's gone," Maddie said the moment the door closed behind Alma's retreating form. She exaggerated a sigh as she flopped down into one of the chairs dramatically.

"She means well," Camilla argued. Far better than some of the families Camilla had been stuck with herself. "I know Alma tends to ramble on and on, but you have to know she cares. If I'm right, you'll have had far worse foster homes than with Alma and Dave."

"Whatever." Maddie shrugged and Camilla watched as the girl began to retreat into her shell again.

Danny laid a hand on Camilla's shoulder, drawing her attention. His voice was low, but the deep tones carried well. "Man, she reminds me of you. Back when we first met, you were so much like her."

Maddie tried to pretend she wasn't interested, but Camilla saw her visibly perk up at the comparison. She'd been working hard to get through to Maddie that she could make something out of herself, despite her origins, but it had been a struggle. Maddie wasn't willing to hear a lot of it. But maybe, oh, just maybe, if it came from Danny, the young girl might start to believe a bit.

"How do you mean?" Camilla asked, although she'd long made the connection herself. She turned mostly toward Danny, but kept Maddie within sight so that she could watch for her reactions.

"Her mannerisms, the way she was flirty with me but standoffish with Alma. And just now, the withdrawing into her own head when you called her out in the slightest." Danny squeezed her shoulder. "You were the same way. Hiding if you could, fighting if you couldn't. More interested in connecting with men than women. All the time hiding your lack of self-confidence behind a mask of indifference."

"I wasn't flirting with you," Maddie argued, but the red in her cheeks highlighted her embarrassment. "You old."

Danny laughed. "And sassy, did I forget to say sassy?"

"You sure he's not your man, Dr. D.? Because he sure seems all touchy-feely for someone you ain't hooking up with."

Camilla's own face heated. Danny's hand still lingered on her shoulder, a warm weight both soothing and disturbing. His fingers tightened just once before he released her, right as her last patient of the day walked in the door.

"Ah, Mr. Jenkins, here for your appointment?" Danny stepped up. "You'd be more comfortable with a male doctor, right?"

"I'm here to see you anyway, Danny."

The elderly man looked over at Camilla and winked. Why, what was that old man up to now? Mr. Jenkins was a real character, and she had a feeling that he was up to something. Mr. Jenkins had been a fixture in Greenbriar for as long as she'd lived in this town. Every day, he wore a flannel shirt with khaki pants. She thought he must have three or four dozen shirts, each with a different plaid. And he wore those shirts regardless of season. It could be pushing a hundred degrees out and Mr. Jenkins would limp by, cane tapping against the sidewalk, his flannel sleeves buttoned firmly about his wrists.

"Patient thief," Camilla whispered under her breath to Danny as she held out the file. She didn't really mind, though. Given that Mr. Jenkins and Robert had been such close friends, she wasn't surprised that he wanted to see Danny instead of her. She thought it might be good for Danny to connect with his father's friend; maybe it would even help him remember who he used to be.

"You can start your weekend early. I'm sure you ladies have big plans that you can get an early start on," he said with a wide grin, taking Mr. Jenkins's chart from her. "Let's go to Exam One, just there on the right, sir."

She watched as Danny followed their patient to the exam room. In the doorway Danny turned and caught her staring.

"I'll see you Monday?" he asked, one eyebrow raised.

Camilla could only nod, heat flooding her cheeks once again. She could control herself better than this. She was a strong, confident physician. She had been running this medical practice alone for some time. Why was she blushing like a young girl in the midst of her first love?

"You got the hots for him then, huh? I seen how red your face got."

"Saw, not seen. You saw how red my face got. And I most certainly do not have the hots for him," Camilla denied. She was a grown woman. A professional. She did not lust after inappropriate men. "And this is a conversation we will not be having, not here, not anywhere."

"Whatever." Maddie rolled her eyes. "You lyin' to yourself if you say otherwise. And for what it's worth, Doc, I think he feels the same way 'bout you."

"What brings you in today, Mr. Jenkins?" Danny asked, eyes skimming over the man's file. Other than age, the man was fairly healthy. No chronic illnesses, only some pain that flared up in winter from an old injury. "If you want to roll up your sleeve, I'll get some vitals on you."

In the month he'd been here, Camilla had hardly let him near a patient without making him work hard for the chance. He'd had to resort to using his charm on the ladies and asking the older men if they'd prefer a male doctor just to have something to do. He hadn't touched a scalpel in weeks and had found himself missing the hustle and bustle of the ER in Boston.

No, he missed having people to talk to.

He'd channeled all his social needs into patient care. Which was a sad but true fact that he'd only become aware of since he came home to Greenbriar. He'd used his patients and coworkers in Boston as a weak replacement for a social life.

"I ain't sick." Mr. Jenkins sat on the end of the exam table and tapped his cane against Danny's knee. "I told you that I'm here to see you."

That wasn't an answer he'd expected to hear and it derailed the line of questions he'd been about to ask his patient, even if he had known the man most of his life.

"I'm sorry?"

"Your father was one of my closest friends." He raised an eyebrow, silently waiting for Danny's acknowledgment of his statement.

"I haven't forgotten." Danny wasn't sure where the old man was taking the conversation, but he remembered the days of sitting between his dad and Mr. Jenkins on the dock, fishing. They'd catch enough for dinner and then sit there gabbing like a cluster of church ladies on a Sunday evening and split a six-pack.

"You gonna break that girl's heart again?" Mr. Jenkins put the question forth with no pretense. No waffling, no beating around the bush. Right to the point.

Danny liked a straight shooter, but maybe not when they got up in his personal business. Whatever happened between him and Camilla shouldn't be anyone else's concern. His hand tightened around the stethoscope in his hand.

Gritting his teeth, he growled out, "Sir, with all due respect—"

"Don't you due respect me, boy. I bet I know what you're gonna say. That it's not my business, right? Well, you keep right on thinkin' that and I'll say what I come to say anyways. Your daddy, God rest him, isn't here to give you this talk, but you need to hear it, and I'm the one here to give it."

Danny took a step back. He wasn't a little boy being scolded for taking a swig of the man's beer anymore. This was his medical practice and, patient or not, Mr. Jenkins didn't have the right to walk in here and talk down to him like he was a child in need of discipline. Stubborn patients, he was used to, but nosy ones were a new one on him.

His spine stiffened and he stared down his

patient. "If you aren't sick, then maybe we should call this a day."

Mr. Jenkins faked a cough. "I'm a paying patient. You want me to tell the state licensing board that you refused me treatment—or better yet, that lovely young woman out in the lobby?"

Danny met the old man's eyes and saw that he wasn't going to back down. And while he gave a brief thought to making a run for it, he sank down on the wheeled stool and waved a hand for him to speak his piece. The deciding factor had been simple—getting this conversation over with would be less drama than avoiding it.

"You didn't see what a mess you made of that girl. How broken she was when you sent her away and skipped town like someone lit your hind end on fire. We did." Mr. Jenkins took a deep breath, as if fortifying himself for what else he needed to say. "We patched her up and made her whole again. We were the ones standing by as she held this practice up alone for the last two years while your daddy was too sick to work. Like Atlas holding the weight of the world, that girl held up your daddy and this whole town on her petite little shoulders. She's got a strength to her that's come from clawing her way out of the pits of a broken heart."

Closing his eyes, Danny stifled a groan. How could he respond to that? He had no way to argue it. There was nothing he could deny in Mr. Jenkins's speech. He hadn't been home in years, because it was easier than risking bumping into Camilla. He'd missed his father's final moments as a result. He hadn't even known his father was sick until after he was gone and to hear, first from Camilla, and now from Mr. Jenkins, that he'd been sick for two years was almost too much to bear.

"And I'm here to tell you that this town will not allow you to break that girl again." Mr. Jenkins jabbed the tip of his cane into Danny's side to drive home his point. "You listening to me, boy?"

Danny nodded nice and slow, pushing the cane down gently. He got the gist of it—the whole town was on Camilla's side and he'd better not screw things up with her again.

"Now, nobody's gonna be unreasonable here. I saw the way the two of you were still looking at each other, and I ain't blind, despite pushing eighty. If you have honorable intentions and want to court the girl proper-like, and if she deigns to give your yellow-bellied butt a second chance, well, that's her business. But know we will all be watching you."

"Yellow-bellied?" Danny shook his head. What did this old man know about anything? Mr. Jenkins had no right to judge the choices he'd made. If only he could get someone to understand why he'd *had* to end things with Camilla... Why he'd had to leave town... If even one person was on his side, maybe the guilt wouldn't be quite as bad. "You don't know anything about me or why I made the choices I made."

"You think I don't know why you broke things off with that girl after the accident? You think I carry this cane for the fashion of it?" He twirled the wooden implement in the air to emphasize his words. "Naw, son. I've been in your shoes. I was the one behind the wheel when a car wreck shattered my thigh and, worse than that, took my only son from me."

That confession made Danny look at Mr. Jenkins with fresh eyes. The man had used a cane for as long as Danny had known him, but never once had he asked why. He never knew Mr. Jenkins had been in an accident, but before he could ask for any details, Mr. Jenkins continued his story.

"You think I wanted to come home to my

sweet Mary Ellen as the man who couldn't protect our baby boy?" A haunted shadow in his eyes backed up the words. He shook his head and then tapped his finger against his temple. "The damage to my leg was nothing compared to the sinkhole that formed up here. The nightmares, the flashbacks. I didn't want to bring that mess back home to Mary Ellen and our baby girl."

Danny found himself intrigued by the man's story and the feelings so similar to his own. Mr. Jenkins's generation didn't talk about things like mental health issues usually, but his words resonated deep. While Danny had walked away from the accident that had killed two of the most important people in his life with comparatively little physical injury other than some shrapnel to one leg, mentally it was a completely different story. He'd felt less than whole, like damaged goods too far gone to contaminate Camilla.

Despite her childhood, Camilla had this goodness about her, this light, that made everyone around her feel better about themselves. He'd known that she would give and give to try to make him whole again, even if it took everything from her, and he had made the decision to spare her that. To not bring his mess back home to her, to borrow Mr. Jenkins's phrasing.

"But you did."

"God help me, I did." Mr. Jenkins stared over Danny's shoulder at an empty patch of wall. Pain left his aged face raw, decades after the time of his tale.

Danny felt that in the depths of his soul. Even after eight years, some days his pain was as raw as the day of the accident. Would he still feel it as keenly as Mr. Jenkins did when he reached eighty? His insides churned with that thought.

"It worked out for you, though, right?" he asked, trying to focus on the positive. Mr. and Mrs. Jenkins had always seemed so happy and in love from his point of view.

"Mary Ellen had the patience of a saint, I tell ya. She got me up when the nightmares got too bad, and she took our daughter to her mama's and came back to take care of me when the darkness pulled me under and I tried my best to drown myself in a fifth of whiskey. Even if I could have walked away from Mary Ellen, telling myself she'd be the better for it, I couldn't do that to my daughter. I'm ashamed to say that my wife had to do her grieving for our son alone because I couldn't be the shoulder for her to cry on. I was too lost in my own guilt and shame."

Danny buried his face in his hands. How many times had he been glad that there'd been no children thrown into the mix? Like Mr. Jenkins, if he and Camilla had had a child, he couldn't have walked away.

"Mary Ellen was stronger than I believed a woman could be and she stood by me through my worst, never once forsaking me. You were wrong if you thought Camilla wouldn't have done the same for you. You were wrong if you thought you were doing her a favor by pushing her away." Mr. Jenkins stood and put a wrinkled hand on Danny's shoulder. He squeezed tight in the way old men do. "And you are wrong now if you can't accept that some things in life we just can't change, no matter how hard we might wish or pray otherwise."

He paused before cracking a grin. "Other things, now, they just need a little sweet-talking."

After warning him off, was the old man actually encouraging him to try again with Camilla? Surely not? It was a moot point, anyway, because she'd never give him another chance. He'd hurt her far too much for that.

"She'd never forgive me for leaving her like I did." He didn't *deserve* her forgiveness.

With a shrug, Mr. Jenkins started out of the exam room. He stopped in the open doorway. "You might want to start with forgiving yourself first, son. Can't ask her to forgive what you can't."

Somehow, he'd ended up being the patient instead of the doctor today. The old man's footsteps and the soft tap of his cane receded and the tinkling of the front bell told Danny he was alone with his thoughts. The magnitude of his poor decisions bombarded him. The worst part was that Mr. Jenkins was right. He was a coward. All those emotions he'd been shoving back for so long were fighting for release. The walls of the exam room felt like they were closing in on him.

Gasping, he tugged at the collar of his shirt. Coils of panic spun out around his heart, squeezing it until his chest hurt with the pain of just keeping his heart beating. He tried to get air into his lungs, falling to his knees on the cold tile of Exam One.

Closing his eyes, he breathed in through his nose, out through his mouth. Each breath grew easier and deeper until he felt strong enough to climb up off the floor. He touched the exam table, pulling a handful of the white paper into his hands and focused on the familiar sound of the crinkle. Every detail of the exam table got a once-over as he concentrated on the single object and pulled himself back to a calm state.

Once he was able, he quickly cleaned the exam room. Turning off all the lights, he locked the door. The painting would need to wait until the morning. He climbed into his truck and a familiar song came on that took him straight back to high school prom and Camilla dancing in his arms. Nope. Couldn't go there while he was driving.

Switching the radio off, he drove out to the lake house. Despite the chilly winter temperatures, he went straight out on the dock. Sinking down on the cold, weathered planks, he stared out over the water. There was no breeze tonight, keeping the cold from being unbearable. Wood smoke hung in the air, carrying over from one of the neighbors' chimneys, the scent another reminder of what he'd left behind here in Greenbriar.

He was supposed to be here for the short term. No connections, no emotions, but somehow that didn't seem to be working out for him. Instead, he had people throwing his past up in his face, reminding him of all his deficiencies. Worse than that, though, was the temptation. Camilla's soft smiles and the way she leaned toward him subtly whenever they talked made him want things he definitely had no business wanting.

"Did you want to destroy me emotionally, Dad?" he asked the sky, bold with streaks of pink and orange. "Is that why you forced me back into Greenbriar and Camilla's life?"

A sob rose up from deep inside him, and for the first time in years, Danny cried. Not a few random tears trekking down a cheek to be swiped away with a single brush of the hand, but deep soul-wrenching cries filled with grief and a longing for what had been lost. The memories of all that had gone swam through the tears, leaving behind an ache that couldn't be filled. His mom. Robby. His dad.

Danny grieved, not only for his parents, but himself, too. The man he'd been before a drunk driver had crossed into his lane and shattered every vestige of the future he'd envisioned for himself. For so long he'd denied himself the ability to miss who he had been. Recently, however, he'd become aware that he no longer liked the man he saw in the mirror each day. He wanted to go back to being the happy-go-lucky guy who had the self-confidence to sweep his girl off her feet. Who had the confidence to risk loving someone and not let the fear that he was no good for them keep him from letting anyone close.

The wind picked up, swirling a pair of leaves around him before landing them in his lap. He wiped his face with the sleeve of his jacket and stared down at the leaves, stems twisted together so tight they'd carried on the breeze as a single entity.

His parents' marriage had been like that. They'd weathered all that they'd come up against, from miscarriages to failed adoptions—until death had finally separated them.

He wanted a love like that.

But loving someone meant taking a gamble. Chancing that his demons wouldn't overpower any love he had to offer. Putting a wager on his ability to protect the ones he loved, when he'd failed so miserably at that in the past. How could he take that risk?

CHAPTER SIX

As CAMILLA BACKED out of her driveway, Maddie sighed over in the passenger seat. Camilla spared a glance at the girl before returning her attention to the road.

"Why can't the weekends be longer, Dr. D.?"

"The older I get, the more I wonder the same thing myself." Camilla turned off her street onto the main road heading toward the new high school. The building that she and Danny had attended had been torn down a few years ago and an apartment complex now stood in its place. A lot of memories—good and bad—had happened in that old building. The grounds of the new apartment complex were haunted by teenage bullies, the ghosts of first loves, and the specters of adolescent heartbreak.

Maddie nibbled at her nails and sighed again. Although they'd had a lot of deep and productive conversations over the weekend, Camilla couldn't help but feel that the young girl had something else on her mind she wanted to discuss. Unfortunately, their time was nearly up, so Camilla couldn't take as long as she usually would to circle around the idea first.

"Wanna talk about it?" she coaxed, getting straight to the point.

"There's this boy…" Maddie let it trail off. *It's always a boy.*

"And you like him?" Camilla gave a small, tight smile. Advice about boys wasn't really her wheelhouse, but Maddie was opening up to her. And that was a huge step.

"Well, yeah. He's a senior and he is *so* cute. I think he likes me, but I'm not sure. He kinda has a reputation for fighting and getting in trouble, but when he's with me, he's not like that."

Camilla started shaking her head. While a senior boy was a far more appropriate crush than a grown man like Danny, he was still not a good choice. Maddie really didn't need a boy who was going to lead her down the wrong path because he couldn't keep himself straight. "I don't think that's a good idea. You are far too young to be dating a senior, honey.

It's very rare for a guy that much older to really want to date a freshman."

"What do you know?" Maddie scoffed. "You ain't got no man."

"I remember being a freshman and falling for a senior boy's lies." Camilla pulled into the still-empty parking lot of the insurance agency. She wanted to be able to make eye contact while they talked, and she couldn't do that while she was driving. She had to tiptoe up to this conversation or risk undoing months of trust-building with Maddie. "I was in your shoes. The cutest guy, a senior to my lowly freshman self. And by some miracle, he liked me." She swallowed as the humiliation of those memories filled her once more. "It was great, for a short while, but after he got what he wanted, he was gone. Then he told everyone in our school about it, and the truth merged with the exaggerations and the rumors. Before long, I was fighting about it on a daily basis and soon I lost my foster home. That's when I ended up in the group home here in Greenbriar. I didn't have the strength I do now, the emotional fortitude to stand up for what I believed in without throwing my fists around. I just desperately wanted someone to love me back, even if it was only for a short while."

Maddie bit her lip and looked away. "But how do you ever know if a boy really wants you or just…that?"

Camilla brushed a lock of Maddie's hair away from her face, hoping that by some miracle she was reaching her in a way that the girl would truly understand. "You make him work for it. If he really wants you, he will stick around and wait until you're old enough."

Maddie grinned. "How long did you make Dr. Hottie wait?"

Camilla snorted. "What makes you think—"

"Oh, come on." Maddie rolled her eyes. "I might be young, but I can sense the vibe between you guys. Plus… Everybody in town has been talking about the two of you. How you used to sneak around together…"

"Danny was my first love." *My only love…*

Looking off into the distance, Camilla tried not to drift too far into her memories. "He was the first boy willing to put in the work to really get to know me. We were friends for a while before I was willing to let him be more. And even once we started dating, it was quite a while before…that…happened. I was a few years older than you are now."

Maddie's forehead wrinkled as she seemed to be digesting Camilla's words. Camilla could almost visualize the thoughts running through the girl's head in that moment. *Does he really like me? Is he just using me?*

"Does that answer your question?" Camilla asked softly.

Maddie nodded. The serious expression she'd had a second ago was replaced by one filled with teasing mischief. "How long you gonna make him wait for it this time around?"

"Hush, you." Camilla put the car into gear and pulled back onto the highway. The kid had some nerve! "You need to worry about your school work, not my love life."

"I've known you a long time, Dr. D., and until he came around, I never once saw you blush. But you blush all the time when you talk about him. I just was thinking that if he still gets to you that much, maybe you ain't over him yet."

Camilla slowed the car to a stop in front of the high school. She looked over at Maddie and said, "I'll take that under advisement. Out you go. I'll see you Wednesday night for tutoring."

"I'll take that under advisement," Maddie mocked as she shut the door.

Camilla waited until the girl had crossed the threshold into the large brick building before driving away. She didn't need a fourteen-year-old girl to tell her she might not be over Danny. She huffed in frustration. She could love him with everything she had and it would never be enough if he didn't return the sentiment and share the same wants in life. She'd learned that the hard way when she'd poured every ounce of herself into their relationship and he'd ended things without even the hint of a warning. And she was no longer that teenaged girl fiercely longing for someone to hold her. Now she had enough self-respect to make the tough choices and delay a quick physical release if it didn't satisfy her emotional needs.

When she parked the car in front of the office, she realized she'd driven the entire way on autopilot. *That was safe, Camilla.*

She grabbed her purse and hurried through the crisp early March air. She kept close to the brick storefronts that lined the street, the buildings breaking some of the wind. She slowed when she reached the medical practice. The sign painted on the front window still read Dr. Robert Owens in large letters, with her name below it in a smaller print. She'd need to change that. Unlocking the door, she stepped inside, where the faintest hint of paint fumes still clung to the air. A lovely gray shade warmed the walls. Camilla gaped as she took it all in. The neutral paint brought such a crisp modern feel to the office, replacing the dated wallpaper with a timeless classic look.

Everything had been put back in its place, ready for patients bright and early this morning. The chairs were lined up along the wall, evenly spaced. Danny had even taken the time to fan the magazines out on the coffee tables.

It was perfect.

"So, how'd I do?"

Camilla jumped, her hand flying up to cover her heart that tried to jump out of her chest. She hadn't realized Danny was already in the office this morning. "Other than scaring the life outta me?"

"Didn't mean to startle you." Danny stood in the opening to the hallway, one hand propped casually on the wall. His faded blue jeans and paint-splattered T-shirt looked out of place in the setting, but oh-so-right on him. Snug denim hugged his thighs and the cotton of his T-shirt stretched tight across his broad shoulders. "What do you think?"

"It's amazing." Camilla spun slowly, letting it all sink in while hoping Danny hadn't caught her staring at his gorgeous form. "The color on the wall is better than I hoped. It's the perfect shade."

When she completed her revolution, Danny was no longer at the edge of the room but right beside her.

"So you like it?" he asked.

She nodded and swallowed hard at his sudden nearness. Knowing he was within arm's reach had her body in a state of wicked awareness. Physical release does not lead to emotional satisfaction—she repeated that mantra in her head as he moved even closer.

"Good." He reached out and touched her scarf with a single finger. "I can't believe you still have this. I would have thought you'd have thrown it in the fireplace."

"I thought about it. But it wasn't the scarf's fault that you bought it for me. Plus, I've always loved it." Every time she'd tried to get rid of the soft cashmere, she'd second-guessed herself. She'd bought other scarves, but none had ever managed to convince her to dispose of this one.

"Even when you hated me?" While his question was barely audible, there was something in his eyes that seemed to be screaming, "Please don't hate me!"

"I've never hated you," she confessed just

as quietly. "Not even when my heart was breaking."

He grabbed both ends of the scarf and tugged her against his chest. Eyes searching, Danny stared down at her for a moment. She was completely unprepared for the feel of his touch. His arms slipped under her coat and held her tight, hands splayed on her back.

Camilla's heart skipped a beat as he lowered his head toward hers. Her hands came up to his chest, feeling the strength in his muscles beneath her fingertips.

The phone in her pocket rang, but they didn't immediately move apart. Slowly, Danny eased back the tiniest bit, barely enough to allow either of them to take a deep breath. They stared at each other. Danny's eyes were full of passion and wonder, and Camilla thought he must be seeing something similar in her own. She couldn't stop the flood of emotions overwhelming her senses in that moment, or that every single part of her was saying, "Kiss him."

Her phone rang again.

"You should answer that," he said, still holding her close.

Removing her hands from his chest to grab the interrupting device, she winced when she saw Alma's name on the screen. She'd forgotten she was supposed to update her when she dropped Maddie off at school. The woman would be frantic.

"Hi, Alma, yes, she's at school. I dropped her off on time. I just got a little distracted and forgot to let you know." Camilla's voice was shaky as she tried to reassure the nervous foster mother that her charge was safe and sound at school, where she belonged. All the while, Camilla remained wrapped up in her ex-fiancé's arms.

Alma fussed for a minute, but then ended the call, thankfully.

"Um…" Camilla bit her lip, not knowing what to do with Danny. His arms remained around her, but the moment had passed, and now things between them felt awkward again. She didn't know if she should step back or wait for him to. They stood that way for a bit, both seeming to want the other to make the decision.

Camilla put her hands up on his chest again, this time to keep him from tugging her closer. Having her hands on him was a temptation, though. Mixed with the familiarity of his embrace was a new vibe between them, something deep and thrilling that hadn't been there the first time around, but it served to make her hyperaware of each spot his body touched hers.

For years, she'd dreamed of the day when Danny would realize the mistake he'd made in letting her go and come back to her, ready and willing to try again. But now that the moment had possibly arrived, she discovered she had far more concerns than her fantasy had ever allowed.

To make things even more confusing, Danny was being so sweet and helpful. He'd made the changes to the office so perfectly that it was as if she'd done every bit of the work herself. And the way he held her had brightened a part of her soul that had remained dim for the better part of the last decade. Yet she couldn't help being afraid of what the future would hold if she let her guard down. What if she inadvertently did the opposite of what he needed once more and he pushed her away again? Could she handle losing him a second time?

"I don't think we should do this," she said finally.

"Yeah, you're probably right. I'm going to head out. I've been here since yesterday getting this place ready for business today. I could use a nap." He stepped back and she watched as he put more than physical distance between them. Barriers dropped down in his eyes as he emotionally blocked himself off from her again.

"Bye," she said softly.

He strode out the door without grabbing his coat and she couldn't help thinking he was running away from her and that earth-shattering near kiss they'd just about shared. An almost embrace that had the power to upend her world. Maybe the potential of it had rocked his axis as hard as it had rocked hers.

Sitting on the edge of the desk, Camilla brought a hand up to her lips. Danny Owens could still shake her to the very core. If she wasn't careful, she was at risk of falling head over heels in love with him again and handing him the ability to destroy her once more.

The problem was, she wasn't sure she could stop it. Especially not when such a simple touch tempted her soul and being in his arms again had felt so much like coming home.

When Danny got to his truck, the realization that he was running away yet again hit him. He turned and leaned against his truck and stared back at the office. Mr. Jenkins's words tumbled forth into his mind, that he'd have to forgive himself first. One of the biggest things he'd struggled to get past was the guilt he carried from all the running away he'd done through the years. He'd run away from Camilla, and from his dad. He'd run at the first hint anyone was ever trying to get close enough to connect with him. He wasn't going to do it again. Wasn't going to pile more guilt onto his already overburdened shoulders.

Squaring his shoulders, he strode back to the office. Visions of how many ways this could go wrong flashed through his head, but he bounced them right back out. He only had headspace for positivity. He might not be able to get through all his past guilt just yet, but at least he could avoid adding to it.

Camilla jumped up from the desk when he walked back in the room.

"I think we need to talk about what just happened." He certainly didn't want to talk about it. Talking would acknowledge the elephant in the room put there by that spontaneous embrace, but he and Camilla were only just landing on solid ground and they had to rebuild their whole foundation. That meant putting it all out there, even if it was miserably uncomfortable. He wasn't running from her again. Not physically, not mentally.

She nodded and gave a weak smile. "That was…unexpected."

That was an understatement and a half. "For me, too."

"Then why?" A deep pink rose up in her cheeks. It made her look even more kissable.

He put his hands in his pockets to keep from reaching for her again. "I could say it was just nostalgia or a heat-of-the-moment thing. But I don't want to lie to you. While it was an impromptu gesture, the feelings that rose up made me wonder if we might still have something there to explore."

"Maybe trying again would be worth it, or maybe I'll get my heart shattered again. What if we are just toxic to each other and this will only end in pain for both of us?" She gave voice to some of her concerns.

He held a hand up and she stopped speaking in response. "I know we have a lot of things to work out. And I know I really don't deserve another chance with you. But maybe we could take some time to get to know each other again, see if there is more there than just a spark of leftover passion."

"Spark of leftover passion..." Camilla echoed his words, her tone suddenly tight and clipped. She sucked in a breath, as if fighting against herself before continuing. "I think we need to focus on the keyword in that sentence—*leftover.*"

"Why are you pushing me away?" They were teetering on the edge of a precipice and one wrong move from either could send them both back into the abyss of anger and avoidance, but he couldn't help taking another step forward.

"I don't feel like I can trust you."

Defensiveness rose swift and sharp in his gut. "What do you mean you don't trust me? Do you honestly think I'd ever intentionally hurt you?"

"You ended our relationship without so much as a conversation. I never got to find out what went wrong, whether things were fixable or not. Nothing. Just 'give me my ring back and get out of my life.' I thought we were fine—I mean, yeah, of course I knew your accident was going to change some things, but I didn't think we were at the point of breaking up forever. I trusted you, more than anyone in my life, ever, and when you threw us away—threw me away—like an empty pop can, then it broke my trust."

An emotional sound, somewhere between a sigh and a sob, escaped her, but she continued her speech. "It made me second-guess everything about myself. I couldn't trust my own judgment, because my judgment had told me you were trustworthy, that you cared about me, and look where that led me."

Reaching out, he cradled her hand within his. He wanted to wrap his arms around her, hold her in his arms and soothe away her concerns, but settled for holding her hand. While he might have lost her trust in one swift moment, it would take far longer than that to rebuild it. Patience would have to become his new best friend. "If it helps at all, I am truly sorry."

"Danny, I…" She trailed off and considered him carefully. He could see the warring emotions that crossed her face.

Before Camilla could answer, the office door opened and slammed back into the wall. A man in blue jean overalls and a dusty ball cap staggered in, his arm ripped open and blood pouring from the jagged wound. The blood on the carpet would never come out, but, thankfully, it needed to be replaced anyway.

"Doc, I think I'm gonna need a few stitches," the man said, wobbling backward and sitting down hard on the table by the door. Medication brochures fluttered to the floor from the impact. The man's face paled. "Boy, this room sure is spinning."

Camilla gaped at the man. "Mr. Hughes, what did you do?"

Danny jumped into action. Finally, a patient he could take point on. Helping the gentleman to his feet, he led him to the exam room. As he gloved up, he called out, "Camilla, I need an irrigation tray and some gauze. How'd this happen, sir?"

"My yard had just started to look shaggy and I was trying to get the first cut of the season in. I sneezed and ran my mower into the dang fence. Barbed wire snapped and got the best of me." He winced in pain as Danny probed the edge of the cut with a gloved fingertip.

Camilla brought the irrigation supplies in and got them set up next to the exam table. "What else do you need?"

"Gotta see what we are dealing with here." He put a gauze pad over the wound and smiled at his patient. "Hold that in place. Give me just a sec to talk to Dr. Devereaux in the hallway, okay?"

He motioned for her to step outside. When the door clicked behind them, he asked quietly, "Do you keep any blood products here?"

"No," she answered back, her voice low to match his own.

"Okay, go ahead and call for an ambulance. I'm going to patch him up as best I can, but this wound needs far more than simple stitches. I need to make sure that there's no nerve damage first and we just don't have the equipment here for that."

When she moved into her office, he hurried back to his patient. "Now, let's flush this out and see where it stands."

A few minutes later, Camilla knocked and came back into the exam room. She was handling this remarkably well given that she normally didn't see blood pouring out of a man in large quantities. This was well beyond her typical cases of strep throat and sinus infections. He had no doubts that if he hadn't been here, Camilla would have taken good care of this patient. If he knew one thing, it was that she was an excellent doctor.

While she was gone, he'd been able to clean the wound and wrap it tightly to slow the blood loss. "I was just explaining to Mr. Hughes here that we need to send him over to County to make sure there's no nerve damage and let them stitch him up."

"Right." She nodded in agreement. "You don't want me to sew you up, Mr. Hughes. I'm afraid I haven't done more than dermal adhesives or a few staples in years. This is a little beyond that."

"I could do it, but I want to have a neurologist take a look first," Danny felt the urge to add. He wanted Camilla to see him as a skilled trauma surgeon, to see that he hadn't wasted all the time they'd been apart, at least.

"Thanks, Docs. I'm feeling pretty woo... woozy," Mr. Hughes stuttered as he swayed on the table.

That ambulance couldn't get here fast enough to suit Danny. This patient needed far more care than they could give him here. They didn't have a surgical suite. Honestly, they didn't even have an X-ray machine, just one old ultrasound machine and an automated external defibrillator. None of which would do much if Mr. Hughes coded on that table.

"Why don't you just relax back here then. Best to lie down before you fall down, don't you think?" Camilla moved quickly to recline the table. She elevated Mr. Hughes's arm and kept talking to him in a soft, crooning voice.

"You sure are prettier than ol' Doc Owens," their light-headed patient muttered, flirting with Camilla.

"Why, thank you!" she replied with a smile, turning that Southern charm of hers on the man.

Her words were having a calming effect on the patient, so Danny didn't want to say anything to distract from that. But he did want to get his vitals. Danny stepped to the other side of the exam table and listened to the man's heart while Camilla kept his attention engaged. His vitals were far shakier than Danny would like to have heard.

"I need to ask you a very serious question, Mr. Hughes," Camilla drawled. "When did you last have a tetanus shot? You and I both know that barbed wire fence around your place has seen its share of rainy springs and has more than a touch of rust on it."

When Mr. Hughes said he couldn't recall, Danny slipped out of the room and retrieved the medication and a syringe. A tetanus booster was always a good idea when rusty metal was involved. He also grabbed an IV kit and a bag of saline. Without blood products, saline was the best alternative he had access to. He injected the vaccine into the man's deltoid muscle on the uninjured arm and set about getting intravenous access established.

"Danny," Camilla said quietly, drawing his attention from the IV he'd just got going. Her eyes flicked to the bandaged wound that was bleeding through the gauze already, even tightly packed and elevated.

He nodded at Camilla and stepped back to the supply closet. He grabbed more gauze pads and a suture kit. As much as he hated to close that wound without a neurologist to check for nerve damage, he had to get that bleeding stopped.

"Okay, Mr. Hughes, we got a slight change of plans here. Since this stubborn laceration of yours insists on bleeding still, I'm going to throw a few stitches in and see if we can't get that slowed down." He moved up next to Camilla, who was still holding the patient's arm in an elevated position. He carefully peeled the bandage back and held back a sigh of relief when blood didn't spurt out at him. He motioned for Camilla to move the limb down onto the irrigation tray. Flushing out the wound with saline again, he scanned the cut for the bleeders.

Finally, he saw the culprit. "Gotcha now, you little bugger." He carefully stitched the bleeding vessel. Stitches weren't always the best choice for that, but when the bleeding wouldn't stop, he didn't have much choice. With that done, he waited to see if there were more, but that seemed to be the biggest source of bleeding. He recleaned the wound carefully before putting in a line of careful sutures.

He once again checked Mr. Hughes's vitals and was pleased to see they were stable now, if a bit weak. His stitches were holding and the bleeding had stopped.

The front bell rang, and Danny couldn't help feeling a little annoyed that the paramedics were there now, after he'd already done the hard work in stabilizing the patient. He directed them to the exam room, rattling off the man's vitals and current condition to the first responders. They soon had the man on a stretcher, wheeled him out of the office and loaded into the back of the ambulance. Hopefully, the surgeon who looked at it wouldn't have to undo all the stitches, but at least the patient would live to reach the hospital.

As the ambulance drove away, their patient safely inside, Danny started feeling the adrenaline crash that always came with the end of a trauma. He flipped the Open sign to Closed, locked the door and carefully stepped around the bloody mess on the carpet. He went looking for Camilla.

She was still in the exam room, trying her best to clean up. He joined her efforts. Side by side, they scrubbed the exam room down in silence. When it was back in shape, they stepped into the hallway.

Camilla took one look at the trail of blood leading from the front door to the exam room and he thought she sighed heavily. But then she closed her eyes briefly and he watched as she visibly summoned that inner strength he so admired.

"Where do you think we should start out here?" She shot him a wry look. "I'm not sure a carpet cleaner will do much, but they rent them over at the grocery store."

Raising one eyebrow at her, he silently begged her to reconsider her statement. Those little rental cleaners would barely make a dent in this mess. They needed industrial-strength machines and chemicals. Or maybe just new flooring altogether.

"I think we need professionals," he finally said.

She pursed he lips. "Yeah, you're probably right on that. I'll call our guy, see how much it will cost to get an emergency clean done as soon as possible. We can't see patients until we get this taken care of."

"I already locked up."

"Good. Could you get the appointment book and reschedule the patients you can? Maybe we can do house calls for the others? Just until we can get the office usable again."

"On it." He went into the lobby, dodging the still-tacky blood on the carpet. He sat at the desk and pulled up the day's appointments and started making those calls. He pushed as many of them as he could back to next week and agreed to do a house call for one elderly woman who sounded like she was hacking up one of her lungs just to have a conversation.

"They are going to send a crew over in about an hour to start on the carpet. I warned them it was bad." Camilla sat on the edge of the desk next to him. "How's it coming with the rescheduling?"

"I'm done. There's only one that I think one of us should do a house call on. She might be more comfortable with you." He gave her the woman's name.

"Her lungs are so bad, but she's determined to stay in her home. I usually go by and check on her every Friday on my way home from work anyways. So I don't mind going out to do a house call for her. Could you stay here and let the carpet cleaners in? They're safe to leave in the building alone and will lock up after themselves. So you can go home after that."

He nodded slowly. "Are we going to talk about what happened earlier?"

"You were brilliant with Mr. Hughes. I'm so grateful that you were here, because I have to tell you, my heart froze at the sight of all that blood. I… Normally, I'd say that I am one hundred percent confident in my abilities as a physician, but my emergency rotation was a long time ago and I haven't had much opportunity—thankfully!—to keep those skills up. Mr. Hughes is lucky that we had a trauma doctor in the building. You saved his life. Can you believe he drove himself here? Stubborn old goat."

"That's not what I meant, and you know it." Danny had to squash the urge to preen like a peacock at her praise, though. She radiated positivity and he was a man starved of upbeat feedback. Having Camilla recognize his hard-won skills sent a balm of peace through him he hadn't expected.

"Oh, that." Camilla laid a hand on his arm. She met his gaze, her eyes filled with confusion and a hint of pink coloring her fair cheeks. "I'm not yet sure how I feel, Danny. I need time. It took me a long time to get over our breakup, and I can't just ignore that."

"I'm not asking you to," he argued gruffly.

"I'm going to go see that patient. I'll see you tomorrow." She squeezed his arm.

"I'll look forward to it." And he found that he really meant that. He'd taken a step forward with Camilla, he thought. And he'd helped save a man's life, while proving to Camilla that he was a competent surgeon.

Today had felt really good.

CHAPTER SEVEN

"REMIND ME AGAIN how we got roped into this?" Danny grumbled, but he hooked another balloon to the helium tank and filled it. He'd already filled a dozen, but there were several more waiting for his attention.

"Because Dave got called in to work unexpectedly and Alma needed help getting ready for Bennie's birthday party." Camilla rolled her eyes. "You know this."

"Correction then, how did *I* get roped into this?" He hooked the next balloon to the machine.

"Because Dave used to be one of your best friends and you are trying to rebuild your relationship with him?" She shrugged. "I don't know your reasons. I'm here because Alma asked me."

He snorted. "And when did you and Alma actually become friends? I know I was gone a long time, but that still surprised me."

"Because as an adult, I realized that Alma is just nervous and talks nonstop as a result. She really has a heart of gold and wouldn't intentionally hurt anyone. She just can't keep a secret to save her life and she has no filter to tell her when to stop talking."

"Hmm." He'd have to take her word for it. He looked around the gaily decorated yard. Crinkle paper party streamers covered in cartoon pirates hung from the fence posts and swayed in the breeze. He'd already set up a series of folding tables and then taped colorful paper tablecloths to each of them to keep them from blowing away in the spring breeze. He'd helped hang a piñata shaped like a pirate ship from a low-hanging limb of a maple tree. "And still, I ask, how did I get dragged into helping prepare for a kid's birthday party on such a beautiful Saturday in April? I could be out on the lake with a fishing pole in hand, enjoying this sunshine from a boat on the water."

"Clearly it was so that you could spend the day with me, of course." Camilla stepped closer, laying her palm on his arm. "And that will make it all worth it, right?"

Danny hissed in a breath as she ran her fingers along his forearm. "Yeah," he said, his voice higher and squeakier than he'd like. Camilla had been flirting with him for the last couple of weeks now, and he was finding her harder and harder to resist.

"I have balloons to fill with helium, woman. Stop trying to distract me." He pushed her back playfully. He kept his tone light. "Alma looks like she could use a hand over there. Go bother her."

"In a minute," Camilla said. "I was wondering if you would mind helping me with the Memorial Day festival at the end of next month. The clinic has staffed a first aid booth there for as long as I can remember."

"You need someone to help you hand out Band-Aids and sunscreen?" He shrugged. "Why not?"

"Great." Camilla beamed at him, making him glad he had said yes.

Over the next hour, he filled the remaining balloons, carried far more presents than one newly four-year-old boy needed to receive outside to the designated presents table, and taste-tested at least three different things for the women who had showed up early to the party. He was fairly sure they all knew their dishes were fine—after all, what Southern woman brought a dish she wasn't proud of out in public. From the way they'd been eyeing him, he was quite certain it was just an excuse to talk to him. He wasn't enjoying the extra attention. The party hadn't even started yet, and he was ready to get out of here.

Yet he stayed.

Because Camilla was there.

Danny found a shaded spot along the fence and sank down into the grass to relax for a bit. To get away from the overtly friendly women of this town. So far, he was the only male in attendance over the age of five. His gaze lingered on the deck where Camilla, Alma and the other women stood talking. Bennie and half a dozen other little ones ran around the yard wearing pirate hats, shouting things like "Ahoy, matey!" just before smacking each other with cardboard swords.

Alma's twin sister, Amy, strolled over with a bottle of water. She held it out to him. "You look like you might have worked up a thirst. Alma couldn't have pulled all this together without you."

"Thanks," he said, reaching up to take the proffered beverage.

Amy held on to it for a moment. "So I was thinking, if you are going to be in town for a bit…" Her words trailed off, but her intentions were crystal clear.

"I'm not sure how long I'll be here. And while I appreciate the, uh, invitation, I'm going to have to pass." He tried to think of a way to reject her politely. His eyes shifted behind her to where Camilla stood watching them. Even from a distance, he saw the stiffness in her posture.

"Man, is that the way the breeze is still blowing?" Amy shook her head. "I thought the two of you had burnt out years ago."

"There's nothing between Camilla and me. But I'm only going to be in town until the start of August. It wouldn't be fair for you and me to start something up now." Danny stood up.

"But it could be fun," Amy said with a smirk, laying her palm on his forearm. Her touch did nothing for him.

"Sorry, it's still a no." He took a step back. "But really, I am flattered by the offer."

Amy looked mad enough to spit nails, so he thought it best to get as far away from her as he could. He stepped up on the deck and took a cookie off the tray there. The sugar cookie he chose was shaped like a skull wearing a red bandanna. Breaking a tiny piece off, he popped it into his mouth. The cookie was buttery and held a hint of vanilla.

"You aren't supposed to be eating those yet," Camilla scolded as she walked over.

"You gonna stop me?" he taunted. He bit another chunk out of the cookie skull.

"Not if you share." She reached out and grabbed a skull cookie of her own. Her pink lips closed over the red frosting bandanna.

"They're good, right?"

"Oh, yeah, they are." Camilla rubbed her thumb along his lower lip. "You have a bit of icing right there."

Danny went to speak, but his voice refused to come. She was trying to kill him. He was certain of it. His lip tingled from her touch and he desperately wanted to kiss her right there.

"Okay, now, you two," Alma called. "Don't melt my kid's cake, huh?"

"Sorry," Camilla said as she took a step back. The bright blush in her face made him feel a little guilty for his part in the flirting, but she had instigated it.

"No, don't be sorry, honey," Amy added with a wry laugh. "If the rest of us had a shot, we'd be taking it, believe me."

Danny cringed inside, but did his best to keep his expression neutral. "When are we going to do cake or presents? I'm sure Bennie's beyond ready."

Alma shook her head at him, her face twisted with the effort of holding back a smile. "You aren't quite smooth enough to pull that change of subject off, Danny Owens, but since it is Bennie's big day, I'm gonna let it slide."

"Well, I think cake sounds like a brilliant idea," Dave said from behind Alma. He nodded at Danny. "I owe you a big thanks for helping to set all this up."

"It was no trouble." Danny shrugged. He didn't want any recognition.

Alma hugged her husband, then turned and shouted out to the kids, "Who thinks it's time for cake?"

Camilla locked her arm with Danny's and led him over to the side. Their part in making sure Bennie's party went well was now done. And she could enjoy herself a bit.

Honestly, it had taken her aback when she'd answered Alma's plea for help and found Danny already in the backyard, wrestling with a folding table. A kid's birthday party hadn't seemed like something he'd want to do, but he had really surprised her in the weeks since that almost kiss at the clinic.

"You want cake?"

"Nah, I'm good. But go grab some if you like."

Danny shook his head. "That cookie was

enough for me. So, unless you want to share one, then I'm good."

"Better not." Her cheeks heated again at the reminder of her brazen flirting. She wasn't sure what had come over her. She only knew she hadn't appreciated seeing Amy approach him like that.

"Too bad," he said. His dark eyes glittered dangerously. Camilla knew she could easily let herself fall back in love with him. Every moment they spent together made it harder to keep her hands to herself.

"Time for presents!" Alma called out, pulling their attention away from the tension between themselves. Maddie and her friend appeared from the corner of the deck where they'd sat whispering and giggling, to surround Bennie as he opened his gifts.

Bennie squealed happily. Soon bits of wrapping paper were flying left and right as the four-year-old tore into his birthday gifts. A gust of wind carried a piece of pastel blue tissue paper through the air toward them. Danny reached out and caught it, disposing of it properly.

Package after package was opened. The presents ranged from a couple of packages of toy cars up to a large block set. Finally, he got to the last present. That one was taller than him and wrapped in plain brown paper with a crudely tied bow around the middle. He ripped into it to find a stack of various sized boxes, a new package of markers and some colorful tapes.

"Oh, wow!" Bennie breathed. "I'm gonna build a rocket ship!"

"Go thank Dr. Owens," Alma said, her voice tight. Camilla worried that her friend was upset that Danny's simple gift had upstaged her much more expensive offerings.

Bennie ran over to Danny and flung himself into his knees. "Thank you, Dr. Owens."

Danny looked uncomfortable for a brief second before returning the little boy's hug. "You're very welcome, buddy."

"Come on! You can help me build it!" Bennie grabbed Danny's hand and pulled him across the yard and put him to work. The little one was like a tiny general ordering both Danny and his father around as a rocket ship was quickly constructed out of cardboard boxes and decorated with tape and markers.

Camilla bit her lip as she watched. The tension in Danny's frame eased and a smile graced his face. He was soon laughing with

Dave and the little boys as they taped boxes together and decorated them.

Alma came up next to her and threw an arm over her shoulder. "It's not my place to say, but I want you to be careful. You've got those same stars in your eyes that you did back in high school. I don't want to see you get hurt again."

Camilla leaned her head against Alma's. "I know. Something about him draws me in like gravity, though."

"Camilla, he broke you. I..." Alma paused and Camilla wondered if her outspoken friend had actually chosen to not speak for once, but then Alma continued. "It took a long time for you to come out of the funk he threw you into. Going down that road again, is that the best idea?"

Camilla let out a long breath. "I appreciate the concern—"

"But you have already made your mind up to give him another shot." Alma gave her a squeeze. "I won't say anything else, then. And I honestly and truly hope that he's not gonna hurt you again. He seems different than I remember. You think he's changed?"

He had definitely changed. But she wasn't going to discuss the whys and hows with Alma, and certainly not in a yard full of people. Danny deserved far more privacy than that.

"Hmm." She made a noncommittal sound, hoping that would appease Alma for now.

Seeing Danny laughing, lying on the ground with a group of preschoolers piling on him like he was a mountain, made her smile, though. One day, he'd make a good father. He was great with kids when he let himself relax.

As the party wound down, people began to leave. She said goodbye to Alma and slipped out the gate.

"Camilla, wait," Danny called from behind her.

She paused and gave him time to catch up.

"Can I walk you home, Dr. Devereaux?"

"I think I'd like that, Dr. Owens."

"I have to admit, that was far more fun than I expected it to be," Danny said as they reached the sidewalk. "I didn't have high hopes for an afternoon spent at a children's birthday party."

"You looked like you were enjoying yourself." She sucked in a sharp breath when he interlaced their fingers as they walked down the sidewalk toward her house. Every touch of his hands brought with it a wealth of old memories and more than a little desire to make new ones. "I haven't seen you smile or laugh that much since you've been back."

"Greenbriar has been more relaxing than I expected it to be."

Camilla faked a gasp and looked around. "Shh...someone will hear you and think you actually like our town."

"We wouldn't want that, now, would we?" His deep voice held a hint of amusement. "I had a lot of fun playing with the boys. I never expected my box of boxes to go over so well. I remember when I was little, my mom and dad used to keep all the boxes that came through the clinic for us. Robby and I would build castles and forts and rocket ships that had medical labels on the side and sometimes we would pretend that was the name of our ship or the location of our castle."

Camilla steeled her nerves against the longing that rose up. She'd never had parents who would have thought to bring her boxes to play with. Her only memories of her biological parents were hazy and involved a lot of yelling. And the worst one of all, the sheer terror she'd felt when she woke up alone and they never came home. She'd never forget the look on the neighbor's face when she'd knocked on her door asking for food and if the neighbor had seen her parents. It was imprinted onto her mind, never to be erased.

"Well, Bennie sure enjoyed it." She forced a smile and a return to happier thoughts.

When they got to her house, Danny walked her up the steps.

"You should go," she said, her voice thick, and the words came out more like an appeal for him to stay than an order for him to leave.

He moved closer, though, pinning her against the front door. "Have I told you today how pretty you look in this color pink?"

"No." Her lips twitched with the effort of suppressing a giggle. Sometimes Danny made her feel like a teenager again, prone to blushing and giggles. What next, was she going to start doodling his name on her files at work?

"Well, you do." He brushed his lips against hers, ever so slightly. It was more of a tease than a kiss, a testing of the waters. When she didn't push him away, he kissed her again. His hands tangled in her hair and his lips moved over hers, soft at first, not tentative, but giving her time to pull back if she wanted to.

She wrapped her arms around his neck and returned the kiss. Her legs felt a little weak and she clung to his shoulders to keep upright.

Then, as fast as it began, Danny ended the kiss. He took a step back and left her grabbing for the doorframe to make sure she stayed on her feet.

"So, uh… Thanks for helping me reconnect with Dave. I needed that more than I knew."

"You are very welcome," she whispered. Was he going to ignore the fact that he'd just rocked her entire world?

"I'll see you soon." Danny whistled as he walked away.

Camilla unlocked her door and leaned against the frame. She had to fight the urge to chase Danny down the street and snatch another kiss.

But what if he leaves again?

With one last, lingering look at Danny, she sighed. Stepping inside, she closed the door. Soon, she would have to really consider whether or not she could handle it if Danny left again.

But for today, she simply wanted to think of that kiss and the feel of Danny's hands on her body as he held her close.

CHAPTER EIGHT

CAMILLA WATCHED DANNY putter around her backyard like he was planning to be there forever. He'd practically jumped at the chance to do her yard work, and given how she'd nearly chopped her foot off last summer when she was mowing, she was hardly going to say no to the help. Being a homeowner was proving to require skills that she had yet to develop.

Thanks to Danny's attention, her front lawn had that manicured look that was usually only found in magazines, and now he'd turned his attention to her backyard. He had visions of turning it into some sort of lush oasis, and she'd loved the sketches he'd made, so she was letting him run with the idea.

Fidget had fallen head over heels for Danny. Camilla thought her pet might even like Danny more than her. Whenever he was around, she wasn't far away. While he worked in the yard, Fidget pranced along behind his every step, her little curly tail wagging nonstop.

Who knew Danny Owens was such a landscaper? Sighing, she gave up even pretending to look at her phone and set it on the porch rail. Danny was far more entertaining to watch than anything she could find on an app. The blue T-shirt he wore stretched tight across his broad shoulders, clinging to the firm muscles of his chest. He'd kept up with most of the physical training from his time as a soldier and it absolutely showed. The cargo shorts he wore were just tight enough on his behind to make watching him walk away a treat. When he bent over to pull some weeds out of one of the planter beds, she had to bite her lip to keep from moaning.

Still, he caught her looking. "Like what you see?"

Camilla did her best to prevent her cheeks from glowing incandescently at the grin on his face. "And if I do?"

His amused gaze met hers. "Good. Because I like looking at you, too."

She'd always had a thing for men who did things for her without being asked, and Danny was certainly filling that well for her. Each and every day, he showed her a little more of the man he was now. He gave her tidbits into his life, into the years they'd been apart, and she wanted more than tidbits. The problem with this was that the six-foot-one, gorgeously muscled man had a "look but don't touch" policy going on. They'd shared that single kiss the day of Bennie's birthday party last month and nothing since.

"Well, aren't the two of you just so incredibly sweet? It makes my teeth hurt even looking at you," Mrs. Sutherland called from where she stood in the open gateway.

"Close the gate!" Camilla cried.

But it was too late.

Fidget caught sight of the opening and bolted through the wide-open gate with glee. Nothing more than a black-and-white blur, she was gone before Camilla could get up out of her chair.

"Fidget!" she cried out, but her beloved pet didn't stop.

Danny hurried out the gate past Mrs. Sutherland after the little dog. He was around the corner and out of sight before Camilla even got off the porch.

On the verge of panic, she moved toward the gate but was blocked by her nosy neighbor.

"Camilla, dear, I stopped by—"

"I really don't have time at the moment."

Patience was also in short supply. What kind of person opened a gate and just stood there with it open?

"I wanted to speak to you about that girl you've had over a few times, the one that Alma Stone's fostering. I think she's falling in with the wrong crowd. I do watch what's going on in this town, you know."

"I'd love to talk to you about Maddie another time, but right now, I need to find my dog." She did want to know if Maddie was going astray, but her immediate concern was for Fidget.

"Pshaw." Mrs. Sutherland waved a dismissive hand at her. She shook her head like Camilla was silly for even being concerned. "It'll come home when it's hungry. And besides, it's just a dog."

Just a dog?

"In case you've forgotten, Mrs. Sutherland, I have no family. That furry little dog is all I have and I love her very much." She glared at the woman as she stepped aside. Normally, she was far more respectful of her elders, but right now she simply wasn't capable of it.

"You're right," Mrs. Sutherland conceded, her face paling at the realization of what she'd done. "I apologize. I really didn't mean to let her out."

Camilla softened. The elderly woman really wasn't the malicious type. Gossipy, yes. A bit careless at times, but she wouldn't do something to hurt someone intentionally. "I know you didn't, but I need to find my dog. Can we talk later?"

"I'll sit on your porch and see if she comes home." Mrs. Sutherland offered. "Go on, find your little furry friend."

Camilla ran out the gate and stopped when she reached the street, trying to decide which way she should go to begin her search. With no way of knowing which way Danny or Fidget had gone, she was nearly paralyzed with fear. She couldn't lose her dog. She just couldn't.

Thankfully, Fidget was not a super-high-energy dog, despite her current display of athletics. A ten-minute spree around the yard once or twice a day suited the little dog, and it suited Camilla just fine, too. When she'd gone to the shelter in search of a pet, she'd been thinking of a cat, because she wasn't a jogger and didn't want a dog with massive exercise requirements. But when Camilla walked past Fidget's cage, heading toward the cat room at the back, the little dog had jumped up on her hind legs, waving, like she was saying, "Pick me!"

And that had been that—love at first sight. Instead of a cat, Camilla came home with a shih tzu who loved to eat trash and anything yucky off the ground, but also loved more than anything to spend a quiet evening curled up in her owner's lap. So, surely, she wouldn't be far away.

"Fidget!" she called, heading toward downtown, along their normal walking path. Maybe Fidget had followed their familiar route and was waiting for Camilla to catch up. She'd probably made it to the edge of the park at full sprint and then run out of energy.

Please let her be waiting for me up ahead.

She ran up the street, shouting her dog's name as she went. Each person that she passed, she stopped to ask if they'd seen a little black-and-white dog, but no one had seen her. Eyes scanning each yard, Camilla got closer and closer to downtown. With each empty yard, the pit in her stomach grew deeper. The alley behind the clinic was empty: no sign of her furbaby.

Walking around the end of the building, she searched the square. Something black-and-white by the back tires of an old truck caught her eye and her heart lurched. Slowly, she moved in that direction. It wasn't moving. When she got closer, she could finally make out that it was a stuffed toy and not her sweet pup. "Where are you, Fidget?"

A sob rose in her throat at the thought she might never hold that furry little body again. Her rescue dog had become more than just a pet to Camilla and she wasn't sure how she'd go on if something happened to Fidget. Self-recrimination rose up within her. She hadn't done enough to protect Fidget. The gate shouldn't open so easily from the outside. She should have fixed it so that not just anyone could get into her backyard.

As the sun sank lower, Camilla's heart grew as heavy as her legs. The fading light left dappled shadows on the ground, creating harder conditions to see a multicolored dog. Her voice was hoarse from shouting out Fidget's name over and over.

What worried her most about her dog being out alone, besides the fear of the shih tzu getting hit by a car, was that Fidget had no sense whatsoever. If a coyote or a bigger dog came after her, she wouldn't back down from a fight. When it came to fight or flight, Fidget got in the fight line twice. She had no concept of being only eight pounds, and would bravely go after something four times her size.

A car slowed next to her. Alma rolled the

window down. "I ran into Danny. He told me about your dog. Hop in and I'll drive us around slow and see if we can find her."

Blinking away tears at the kindness of the gesture, she climbed in the front seat next to Alma. "Thank you for this."

"Of course." Alma put the car in Drive again and they cruised slowly up and down the streets. Quietly at first, but before long, Alma's natural tendencies to talk became too much to contain, and the flow of words began. "It's the least I can do given all the help you have given Maddie in biology this year. You might not remember, but I didn't exactly ace science. I've always been more of a history buff."

"Anything for Maddie." Camilla sighed. "Mrs. Sutherland had actually come over to talk to me about her, but I put the conversation off to find my dog. She's worried about some of Maddie's friends or something."

"Oh? I have to admit, I've been worried, too. Dave and I try to give her structure— I think kids need structure, don't you?—but I worry that if we push her too far, she will hate us more than she already does. She's so angry, though."

"Mmm…" Camilla mumbled in agreement.

"If we thought she'd be okay with it, Dave

and I would like to adopt her. Bennie loves her, and she's really good with him."

"Adopt?" Camilla whispered.

"Yes, is it a bad idea?" Alma slowed to a stop in front of Camilla's house. She flashed Camilla a look of remorse. "I'm sorry, I need to get home and get Bennie tucked in."

"Thank you for trying, at least," Camilla said earnestly. "It really means a lot that you would take time out of your evening to help me."

Reaching over, she took Alma's hand in hers. When she spoke, she chose her words carefully, not wanting what she said to sound at all discouraging or accusatory. "And if you are certain that you want to adopt, I think it could be a really great thing. Ask Maddie what she feels about it. But be absolutely certain of your decision before you speak to her. Not much is harder for a foster kid than the hope of a permanent home being snatched away because the parents changed their minds."

It hadn't happened to her, but she'd seen the disappointment and the anger more than once with her temporary foster siblings. She'd watched as the hope of adoption faded until they were as hard and jaded as she was. Adoption had never been an option for her.

Her parents had hated her just enough to keep the potential that they might come back for her on the table, which meant no permanent placements.

Alma reassured her that they wouldn't change their minds, but that they would be careful how they broached the subject with Maddie. Camilla hoped Maddie would be open to what a great thing being adopted by the Stones could be for her. To have a stable, permanent family? Oh, what Camilla would have given for that at Maddie's age.

Camilla stepped out of the car and watched as Alma drove down the street.

Mrs. Sutherland sat in the rocker on the front porch. "Camilla, honey, there you are. I haven't seen any sign of your dog. I'm going to mosey on home now. Again, I'm sorry about letting your dog out. Stop by some-time this week and I'll share my concerns about that foster girl."

"Good night, Mrs. Sutherland," Camilla called over her shoulder as she looked under the bushes at the front of the house. She walked around the side, hoping maybe Fidget had come home but was hiding from Mrs. Sutherland. Sadly, there was no sign of her.

Or Danny.

Camilla let herself in the house and got

a drink of water for her parched and achy throat. Where had she left her phone? Maybe it was still on the back porch…

Yes. She picked it up and saw eight missed calls from Danny. Hitting the button, she returned his call.

"Hey, babe," he said as he answered, and then she heard a clatter. "Hang on, I dropped you," he said, his voice sounding distant.

Smiling, she waited for him to pick the phone back up. She finished her water and placed the glass in the sink. Digging under the sink, she looked for a flashlight. There was one under there somewhere, she was sure of it. It was getting dark and she couldn't search for Fidget without light.

"Okay, sorry about that. I've got my hands full here and couldn't hold on to my phone and your squirming mutt at the same time. You could have told me she doesn't like to be carried."

"What?" A tear trekked down her cheek.

"Fidget. Did you know she isn't a fan of being carried?"

"Yes. You…you have her?"

"Yeah, I found her about twenty minutes ago. She was begging for pepperonis from some kids having a pizza party out at the skate park."

She'd been circling the kids, barking and sitting up on her hind legs so that she could beg like a lunatic for bits of pepperoni or pizza crust. The kids had found her hilarious and wanted to keep her. Two brothers had even convinced their mom to take the dog home with them. He'd never tell Camilla that they'd been discussing what they might name her dog.

Thankfully, Fidget had responded to him and come running over when he'd called her name or they might have had an issue. As it was, he'd had to endure a lecture about letting his dog run free and disappointing young children as a result of his irresponsibility. But, he'd chosen to be the bigger person and not cause a scene in front of a group of kids. Who just decided they would keep an obviously well-loved dog with a collar on like that anyway?

The little mutt in his arms wiggled and he almost dropped her. Again. "Hold still, Fidget," he grumbled. "She's determined to make me drop her. I swear."

"She likes to use her legs." Camilla's voice was thick with emotion. He wasn't used to hearing tears in her voice. Anger, yes. Uncertainty, sure. Pain, too often, unfortunately. But not this.

"Are you crying?"

"No," she said with a sob. Sniffles came through the line as she struggled to get herself under control. "Why would I be crying?"

"Babe…" The endearment slipped past his lips before he could stop it. What could he say that would make things better for her? He'd thought she'd be happy he found her dog. Were these happy tears? Impossible to tell over the phone.

"Where are you?"

"I'm at the end of the street. Fidget and I will see you in a minute, maybe two." Danny hung up the phone and roughly shoved it into the pocket of his shorts, all the while trying to maintain his hold on the shaggy little dog in his arms. Having made the mistake of letting her down once, he wasn't falling for that again. The yappy thing had run circles around him for five minutes, teasing him until he got his hands on her again.

Before they got halfway to the house, Camilla ran up to them. She snatched Fidget from his arms and hugged the little dog until it squeaked. Standing in the middle of the street, she held the dog close and just sobbed. The outpouring of emotion made quite the spectacle in the middle of the street. He thought it was a pretty sweet scene, though.

"Might wanna let her breathe. I didn't spend the last two hours looking for her just so you could squeeze her to death." He put an arm around Camilla's shoulders and turned her back toward her house. "Let's get you both home."

Camilla was crying so hard he doubted she'd have made it home without his assistance. Her face was buried in the dog's fur and she let him guide her completely down the street.

The trust she showed him in that moment humbled him. She was allowing him to direct her down a public street, trusting he'd protect her from any traffic. He hoped maybe one day she'd trust him like that in all aspects of her life.

When they got inside, she carried Fidget to the couch while he locked the door. She sat, never releasing the dog. Her sobs cut him to the core. Trying not to disturb her, Danny eased down next to her. Wrapping his arms around her gently, he did his best to comfort her.

"I could have lost her," she cried, still cradling the squirming dog like a baby.

"But you didn't." He brushed a lock of hair away from her tear-dampened face. Camilla never cried like this. She'd always been the strong one, the one people leaned on. To see her fall apart was hard. "She's right here. Safe and sound."

"I need you to put a lock on that gate as soon as you can. No one should be able to open it like that." There was a desperation in her eyes he couldn't deny. He could see that she needed this something fierce. Getting a lock on that gate was now *her* first priority. She begged, "Please, Danny."

"First thing in the morning. No, tomorrow's the festival. But I promise you, the first chance I get, I'll take a look and see what options we have." He'd have to try to squeeze in a trip to the hardware store this weekend. Even if it was a chain and padlock until he could find a more permanent solution for her.

She nodded at him. "I can't lose her again."

"You won't," he reassured her, even though it was a promise he couldn't be sure he could keep. But if there was something he could do to help make sure her dog didn't get lost again, he'd do it. "Has she run off like that before?"

Camilla swiped at her tears with the back of her sleeve. "Not like this. She normally runs circles around me just out of reach until she tires out."

Chuckling, he scratched the dog's ear. "She

did that to me, too. After I got her, she wiggled so much that I had to sit her down so that I could readjust my grip. She got away from me and did loops around me for a good five minutes until I could get a hold of her again."

"She's a punk." Camilla smiled, giving the pup another squeeze.

"How long have you had her?"

"About a year." Camilla relaxed into his side, so much of the tension now gone from her body. "I meant to get a cat, but look at this face."

"You're really attached to her, huh?"

She nodded. "We are a package deal now."

"I see that. First pet?"

"Is it that obvious?" Her smile was shy when she looked up at him.

"Little bit, yeah." He shrugged.

"She's all I've got."

It made more sense now just why she'd gotten so upset about the dog's disappearance. With no family, and no serious relationships, the little mutt had become Camilla's family. She was such a loving person, and in the absence of a human to love, she'd focused all her attention on this furry rascal.

She had him now, too, a human in need of her loving attention. And he was going to make sure that from now on she knew she had someone in her corner. Some might say they'd had their chance, but since they'd crashed and burned, they should leave well enough alone. But the truth was, they'd been solid until he'd let his insecurities and the trauma of the accident come between them. Maybe this was their chance at finally being whole again.

His fingers tangled in her hair as they snuggled on her couch, just the two of them and her dog. The riot of emotions normally swirling through his brain was calm tonight. Between the two hours of walking, and even more so, having Camilla in his arms, his mind was blissfully quiet. He couldn't remember the last time he'd been so at peace.

"I always laughed at people who said their dogs or cats were their kids. Now look at me," Camilla said suddenly, snorting in amusement at herself. "I completely lost it when Fidget got out. I was rude to Mrs. Sutherland, and I'm never rude to my elders. Alma came seeking me out, and didn't even talk my ear off, so I must have looked pretty bad. It's been such a weird night, all because of an open gate."

Danny shrugged. "Mrs. Sutherland will get over herself soon enough. She likely just wanted to flap her lips a bit anyhow."

Camilla shifted so that she could stare at

him, a wide grin on her face. She shook her head, still smiling from ear to ear.

"What?" he asked, his lip curling up slightly in response to her smile.

"Did you hear what you just said?"

His forehead wrinkled as he thought about his words. "Oh, man. What have you and this town done to me? You'll have me saying *ain't* and *y'all* again before summer is out."

After years away from Greenbriar and the southern part of the country, he'd slowly eliminated some of those country colloquialisms from his speech. A few months back home and in Camilla's presence and the words rolled off his tongue like he'd never stopped using them.

"I think it's adorable," she drawled, exaggerating her own accent.

"You would."

Fidget jumped down, and for a minute, Camilla tensed up like she was going to follow her. But then she lay her head on his chest and sighed.

"Thank you again for finding her."

"Anything for you."

"It means the world to me. She's…she's my family. And I would be lost without her. Knowing that you spent your evening looking for her, on foot no less, shows me how invested you are in rebuilding my trust. If you hadn't helped me look for her tonight, you'd have ruined any chance of that."

"You needed me."

He was slightly stung at the implication he might not have helped her, but he knew he deserved it. He hadn't always put her needs before his own in the past. If he wanted Camilla back in his life, it was something that would have to change. Work and more work had been his entire existence for so long. His life had been so monotonous and he hadn't even noticed. Day in, day out, he'd let the busyness of the medical tent or emergency department distract him from anything more personal. But with Camilla, he wanted it all. He wanted the laughter and the arguments and even the tears.

Camilla's finger tapped on his nose. A lock of her hair fell down in front of her eyes and she brushed it away in annoyance.

"What?" he asked, blinking.

"Where'd you go?"

Shaking his head, he pulled her close once more and tried to explain away his lapse in attention. "Babe, if you said anything just then, I'm going to be honest, I wasn't listening. I was thinking about how different my life is here in Greenbriar, with you."

She huffed. "Good differences, I hope."

"Yeah." He gave her a squeeze, laughing when she grunted and slapped his stomach playfully. He pushed the envelope a little more and tickled her side.

"Don't…" she warned, raising up, her eyes glittering.

"Fine." He glanced at his watch and sighed. If he left right now and went straight home he could get a possible five hours of sleep at the most. "I should probably be getting home. It's late and I have to be at the clinic early to pack up supplies for the festival tomorrow. The town council want us set up and ready for potential patients by nine."

Some of the sparkle left her eyes when he mentioned leaving. "Okay," she said softly, but it was her tone that set him to aching.

He searched her face, seeing the disappointment etched there. He wanted to stay. Of course he did. But he wanted to do things right and that meant taking his time. Denying her had to be one of the hardest things he'd done in years, though.

Touching his thumb to her cheek, he gently smoothed it down to trace her lower lip. She had a mouth that was meant for kissing. "We don't need to rush this."

"I know." Eyes closed, Camilla leaned into his touch.

"You know, I don't have to leave just yet." He brushed his lips over hers. "I have time to at least give you a proper goodbye."

CHAPTER NINE

ON MEMORIAL DAY MORNING, Camilla sat on her back porch alone, enjoying the quiet of the early hours. She'd always been a morning person, up by sunrise without a complaint, so that she could have a few moments of alone time while in a crowded foster home or group home. Even once she'd moved out on her own, the habit of being an early riser lingered, and was perhaps too engrained in her personality to change now. Even if she and Danny had been up until the wee hours of the night talking.

The years that had passed when they were separated had shaped them into different people than the young couple who'd broken up that day in that hospital room. Camilla could certainly admit that she'd been changed by her experiences and she was learning a lot about the man Danny was now. The Danny she'd intended to marry had been light and carefree, not this serious, sometimes brooding man that she found equally intriguing.

In other ways, things remained as familiar as always. Danny remembered just how to make her laugh and even recognized when he'd pushed her a little too far. And each touch of his hand was both deliciously familiar and excitingly new all at once.

Every day, she knew she was falling deeper and deeper into love with him. And that honestly scared the snot out of her. He hadn't told her yet what his plans were come August 1. Would he stay? Would he go? One way meant the possibility of having nearly everything she'd ever wanted—her own medical practice and a loving partner to share her life with. The other? Well, she didn't want to think about what she'd do if Danny disappeared from her life again.

Finishing the last dregs of coffee from her mug, she called Fidget inside and shut the little dog in her crate for the day where she'd be safe. She had to get downtown. She needed to help Danny set up the first aid booth before the festivities got underway.

When Camilla made it downtown, all the vendors were already there and a small crowd was gathering. At the edge of the park, she could see the fireworks display being set up.

The town always did a massive pyrotechnics display for Memorial Day. It was one of her favorite parts of the celebration.

The sweet scent of funnel cakes wafted over on the breeze and took her straight back to high school. One of her first dates with Danny had been to come to this festival. They'd shared a funnel cake that day, too. Wistfully, she let the memories of that day rush over her and she could almost feel the giddy hopefulness her younger self had felt when *the* Danny Owens—elite quarterback and star of the dreams of every girl at Greenbriar High School—had held her hand as they walked through the booths together. It was the day she'd started to fall in love with the handsome dark-haired boy who'd had no idea how harsh life could be, and the day he'd begun to show her that not everything in life had to be hard.

True love existed, she really believed that, because of Danny. He'd opened her eyes to possibilities she'd never thought achievable. It was because of him and his family that she'd found her calling as a doctor. She'd never have dreamed as big as medical school without them. She was a poor foster kid, and her ambitions had been much more modest and geared toward independence. They'd showed her that her situation didn't have to affect her future, and more than that, they'd proved how important the love of a family could be. Before Danny had snatched it all away and that family had shrunk to just her and Robert.

She shook herself to clear those negative thoughts that persisted on creeping in. Today was not a day to dwell on the past. She had far too much to do in the present.

When she got close to the first aid tent, she could see that Danny was already there. She stopped for a moment to watch as he worked. He had a pale blue T-shirt on with the Greenbriar Medical logo stretched snug across his broad chest and khaki cargo shorts. She'd noticed he had a thing about needing pockets now and he carried so many things in them that she teased him frequently about retroactively becoming a Boy Scout.

From her position, she could see that he had boxes of gauze, antiseptic and cold packs already set up under the counter. He was organizing the next large box of supplies when he looked up and they made eye contact. Nerves danced around in her stomach as their eyes met.

Pull it together, Camilla. You aren't sixteen with a crush anymore.

When she walked up to the booth, he came

over to greet her. "Good morning," he said, wrapping his arms around her. "It looks like it's going to be a perfect day for the festival. Sunny, but not blazing hot. I grabbed far more supplies than I think we will need, but could you look through and see if there's anything I missed while I have time to run back to the clinic and grab things? I like to be prepared."

"Mmm." She snuggled into his arms, enjoying the security of his arms wrapped around her. So they'd only shared a few kisses and cuddles so far, but it had given her the time to work through what she loved about him. And the strength in his arms making her feel safe was only one of them, even as a small part of her persisted in warning her that getting too comfortable in his embrace would only lead to further heartache. "I think we have time to say a proper hello first, don't you?"

"A proper hello, huh?" He leaned down, smiling. His lips grazed against hers as he asked, "What's a proper hello to you?"

Sliding her arms up and around his neck, she initiated the kiss. Pressing herself against the firmness of Danny's chest, she sighed when he deepened the kiss. When his fingers rubbed in small circles over the small of her back, she settled further into his embrace.

Nothing more than a scraped knee ever happened in Greenbriar anyway, so why did they need a fully staffed first aid booth?

A catcall from right behind her ruined the moment. She wanted to cry when the kiss ended abruptly. It had been such a perfect kiss, too. The interruption was almost a tragedy.

Pulling away with real reluctance, Camilla turned to see Maddie and Alma standing there with matching smirks on their faces. Alma raised one perfectly arched brow and shook her head in amusement. Camilla rolled her eyes and bit back a smile. Then she made the mistake of looking over at Maddie and the sparkle of amusement in the girl's irises was too much, and she felt the heat rising in her cheeks.

Camilla cleared her throat and had to force down the urge to apologize. What did she have to be sorry about? She was a grown woman. While it was a little display of PDA, they'd kept it PG-13 at most. They were barely even PG-13 in private these days.

"Good morning, ladies," Danny said from behind her, his tone casual and unbothered by the fact they'd just been caught practically making out. Even when they were teenagers, he'd never gotten flustered when someone busted them, though. He'd always been so cool and calm about it. "Are either of you in need of first aid?"

"No, I was actually hoping that Camilla could be Maddie's check-in person today?" Alma put a hand on Maddie's shoulder and Camilla couldn't help noticing that this time, the girl's posture didn't stiffen at the touch. "She wants to spend time out here with her friends and Bennie's just too small to be at the festival all day, especially in this heat. I don't want to treat her like a toddler, of course, but I'd feel better if she had someone here to come to every hour or so, to make sure everything is still okay."

Camilla had a no ready on her lips, because her focus needed to be on the first aid tent, but the pleading in Maddie's eyes stayed her refusal. Gosh, she was such a sucker for this kid and her sad eyes. Nodding slowly, Camilla agreed to be a sort of chaperone. "That's fine, but she will have to come to me, and if she doesn't check in, the best I can do is let you know, Alma, and you'll need to follow up."

"Thanks, Dr. D." Maddie rushed forward and hugged Camilla hard, nearly knocking her off her feet in her enthusiasm. "I promise I'll check in every hour on the dot."

"You better."

"You are the best!" Maddie said with a big grin. She looked a little shy and whispered to Camilla, "Alma and Dave said they want to adopt me. I won't screw that up."

"I know you won't." Camilla could tell Maddie didn't want to make a big deal of her potential adoption, so she let the subject drop. Glancing down at her watch, Camilla said, "It's nine forty-five now, so I expect you to check in by eleven or I'm texting Alma at one minute past."

With a sassy salute, Maddie ran off to join a group of teens who had gathered around a booth with virtual reality headsets and games. Teenagers were the same no matter how many years had passed. They liked the newest technology and to avoid adults.

Camilla watched the group fondly. She could only hope they didn't get into as much trouble as she had at that age. At least in such a small town, someone would usually be keeping an eye on them and wouldn't let them get into too much mischief. Hopefully.

Alma reached out and laid a hand on Camilla's forearm. "Thank you, truly. I'm trying to give her a little more freedom, but not too much. As you know, it's a delicate balance with her."

"No problem," Camilla reassured her, although it was a distraction she didn't need that day. But it was a small enough favor that helped both Maddie and Alma, so she hadn't felt that she could refuse.

"You could have said no," Danny said as Alma walked away. He seemed to be reading her thoughts again.

"Could I, though?"

"I suppose you couldn't. I would have." He shrugged, but the grin he flashed her was not so nonchalant. "But no one expects me to be nice all the time. In fact, if I were nice all the time, people would start getting the wrong idea. They might start to think I liked them or something equally as horrid."

He faked a look of fear.

Rolling her eyes, Camilla sorted through the remaining boxes, double-checking what Danny had brought. He'd overprepared, if anything. Danny had brought the basics, along with doses of epinephrine, pressure bandages, arm and leg splints, and their portable defibrillator and various other supplies. Last year, she'd only used antiseptic, a handful of adhesive bandages, and a couple of cold packs. Mostly she'd handed out bottled waters and made people sit in the shade for a bit until they'd cooled off.

"I think you brought our entire supply closet out here. I can't think of a single thing you missed." She nudged him. "You know you are in Greenbriar, right?"

"I wasn't sure what we would need and trust me when I say that I'd rather have too many supplies than not enough." Shadows darkened his eyes. Visibly, he withdrew to someplace she couldn't follow.

Concern welled up inside her. She stepped closer and touched his cheek. "You okay?"

"Hmm." He blinked rapidly as he returned to the present. "Sorry, got lost in my head there for a second."

Camilla wanted to ask. Maybe one day he would trust her enough to tell her about his darkest days. So far, most of their conversations had been light and fluffy; the deepest ones still didn't touch his time overseas or what he'd gone through over there. He'd never once talked to her about the day his mom and brother had died, either.

"How's this festival looking compared to the ones in the past?" Danny reclined against the counter. He stared out over the growing crowd.

She hopped up on the counter and sat next to him. Pointing at the VR booth they'd seen Maddie run toward, she said, "The tech booth is new this year. Mrs. Sutherland and her friends have had that quilting booth next to it since we were coming here as teens. Not sure what that pink glittery tent is on the far side of Mrs. Sutherland. I can't read the sign from this angle."

Danny shook his head. "I didn't know tents could sparkle, but that thing's blinding when the sun hits it just right. It reminds me of the way the sun shimmered on the sand in the desert."

All around them, townsfolk were coming out to shop at the various booths lining the street and leading into the park. Most of the town's older women clustered around the quilting booth, gossiping. When Mrs. Sutherland saw Camilla look her way, she held up her hand and tapped at her ring finger with a smile.

Nosy old busybody. She and Danny would move forward when and if they were both ready. Not based on the teasing or pushing of some old woman who probably didn't even remember what romance was.

"You know what I don't see?" Camilla searched the booths to be certain. "Pam's Popsicles."

"Oh, man." Danny straightened up, eyes scanning through the crowd and searching each of the booths and trailers. Disappointment lined his face. "That's such a bummer. It was one of the things I was looking forward to today. I was thinking it would be a good trip down memory lane for us. Do you remember? Our first kiss was Pam's Popsicles–flavored—Red, White and Blueberry, to be exact. Over by that big oak tree at the Maple Street entrance to the park."

"You remember that?" An affectionate rush of emotions swept over her. The little details that meant so much. Danny recalled them all and it made her all mushy and gushy about it.

"Remember it?" He picked up her hand and laced their fingers together. His palm was warm again hers. A simple act, hand-holding. But it was a connection, an intimacy, that she couldn't get enough of. "A couple summers ago I got a blueberry snow cone and it brought all the memories back, taking me in my mind to Greenbriar and that kiss. I almost broke down and called you that day, but I talked myself out of it, convinced that you wouldn't want to hear from me."

With her head leaned against his shoulder, Camilla sighed. How many times had she wished he would pick up the phone and call? Or prayed he'd be standing at the door when an unexpected knock came? "I wish you had. I've always wanted to hear from you. Of course, given how things ended, I could never be the one to make first contact. The scraps of my remaining pride wouldn't allow it."

"Camilla, I—"

Whatever words Danny had intended to utter were drowned out by a series of resounding booms. Before Camilla could look around to find the source, Danny had thrown her to the ground, his hard body landing on top of her. Pinned between the grass and Danny's chest, Camilla could barely breathe. The horrible sounds coming from the direction of the park sent a shiver of fear down Camilla's spine.

"Danny, I don't know what just happened." When the screams for help started, it galvanized her into action, though. "People are hurt. I need you with me."

Slowly, they rose to their feet, side by side. As she gazed out over the grassy area that had only minutes ago been filled with laughter and smiles, she recoiled in horror at the scene in front of her. Tears filled her eyes as she took it all in.

"Wh-what on earth?"

CHAPTER TEN

THE CARNAGE IN front of him matched his memories of war. All that was missing was the rapid sound of gunfire and the rotors of the chopper stirring up sand all around them. He stood, briefly frozen, watching as people started picking themselves up off the ground, tears and blood running down their faces.

"Danny…" Camilla's hand reached for his. There was an unusual sweatiness to her palm and a slight shake to her hand. "Where do we start?"

He focused on the hand holding his. Camilla need him to be strong today. With zero experience in field medicine, Camilla needed him alert so that he could guide her through whatever had just sent a rude awakening through their sleepy little town.

Resolve strengthened, he pulled her close, pressing a hard kiss to her mouth. Handing her some gloves, he pulled some on himself.

"We get through this one patient at a time. Triage first. The minor stuff waits while we treat and assess worse injuries. Call 911 and tell them we need as many ambulances and medevac choppers as they can send."

Grabbing a couple of tarps, he carried them out and spread them in front of the tent. People were starting to make their way to them for help. "These tarps are for serious injuries only. If you just have minor cuts, I'm going to need you to step aside."

Two men carried a third man over and put him on the tarps, his entire front bloody. "The fireworks, they went off early. Rick said they saw a bunch of teenagers messing with them. They must have jacked the timer or something. Nothing was supposed to go off until at least eight o'clock. He went over to scare the kids off, but before he made it all the way, some of them started exploding. He caught something to the chest. Didn't see what."

"Rick? Just lay still as you can. I'm going to do what I can to fix you up." Danny moved quickly, using his pocketknife to slice the remnants of a cotton T-shirt away from the man's torso. He grabbed a stack of gauze pads and pressed them to the worst of the gaping wounds. Working fast, he pulled them away quickly and tried not to wince when he saw how bad the damage was. With no surgical equipment, no blood products, and no hospital close, this man's chances were slim. Danny packed the wound, taping it tightly and hoped that would slow the bleeding enough to allow the medevac chopper to arrive. He quickly bandaged the other wounds that were bleeding significantly. He asked the men who had carried Rick over to hold pressure on the wounds as best they could. "All right, Rick, that's all I can do right now. I'm going to see if any of your buddies need to be patched up."

Hurrying away felt like the coward's way out, but he'd seen enough similar injuries to know that Rick was about to ask him if he was going to make it. Scars already crisscrossed Danny's soul from all the lies he'd told to soldiers about how they were going to be just fine. He wasn't sure he had it in him to tell that lie again today.

Ripping his gloves off as he walked back to the tent, he tossed them in the small trash can he'd brought over from the clinic. It would never be big enough. Camilla had joked he'd brought the entire supply closet, but he was worried they wouldn't have enough to last them until backup arrived. He quickly poured sanitizer on his hands and grabbed fresh gloves and more gauze and bandages.

Sparing a quick glance at Camilla, he decided she didn't need him for the patient she had in front of her. Instead, he moved on to the teenager that Maddie and another boy were leading over.

"Dr. Owens, he needs help bad," Maddie said as they got close. Her words were rapid-fire, verging on panic as she blurted out everything she knew about her friend. "One of those fireworks shot him right in the chest. It didn't explode or nothing, but then another whacked him right upside his head! It took him clear off his feet and he hit that ground so hard. He don't seem to be breathing right and I don't know if his ear is still on his head."

Danny already had his stethoscope on the boy's chest. Breath sounds were diminished. The boy had air escaping into his chest cavity. He grabbed a pile of gauze and slapped it over the mangled remnants of the boy's ear and wrapped some tape around his head to keep it in place. Head wounds bled profusely. If the boy survived this, he'd carry the scars for the rest of his days.

"Let's sit him down over here. Keep him sitting up, though, okay?" He waved toward the tarps where Rick lay, his chest moving up and down in a ragged pattern. "I need to grab some supplies."

He really did not want to have to deal with a pneumothorax in the middle of Greenbriar's Memorial Day festival, but it didn't look like he had much choice. He hurried over to the first aid tent and riffled through the box of miscellaneous supplies. He had brought some empty needles, he was sure of it. Finally, he found the target of his search.

He hurried back over to the boy and checked his lungs one more time before he uncapped the needle, pulled the plunger free, and jabbed the needle between the boy's ribs. The sudden hiss of air and the boy's gasping breath told him he'd gotten it right. He taped the needle in place with gauze around it.

"Maddie, I need you to stay right here with your friend. If he stops breathing, if he starts breathing in a weird way or making any unusual noises, shout out for me or Camilla immediately, okay? Don't let him pull this out. If he does, he could die."

Maddie nodded, fear filling her eyes, but she sank down on the tarp next to her friend. Danny hated to walk away on that sort of statement, but he didn't have the time to coddle her, particularly when there was a good chance her buddy there had caused all this destruction.

As he began to approach a woman with some shrapnel lodged in her shoulder, Camilla called out for him and he ran over to her side. She was crouched next to a teenager, another from Maddie's crowd earlier. Camilla was holding his hands while he struggled against her.

"He's trying to pull the splinters out. But is that the best idea?" She looked at Danny for confirmation.

The boy had multiple chunks of wood lodged in his arm and one in his cheek. If Danny had to hazard a guess, one of the large mortars had hit a wooden booth and turned it into shrapnel.

"These three we can take out, shouldn't be any issue." Danny pointed at a few of the wood slivers. "But those are far too close to an artery for me to feel comfortable pulling them out here in the field."

He leaned over and made eye contact with the boy, who couldn't have been more than sixteen. "Listen to me. I need you to lay still. I will take out the pieces that are safe to come out. But the others, they need to stay in until you are at the hospital. If you pull them out, and one of your arteries is damaged, you will bleed to death. We have no blood products, no surgical equipment here. There isn't a single thing we'd be able to do but watch you die. Do you hear me?"

The boy nodded ever so slowly, his body growing still as he stopped fighting against Camilla. His eyes filled with pain, tears, and more than a little fear. Danny shrugged off the guilt that came with being so blunt with an injured young boy, but he didn't have time to sugarcoat things to keep the kid from hurting himself even more than he already had.

"Okay, then. This is going to hurt. On the count of three… One…two…" *Yank.*

The kid whimpered but didn't cry out. He glared hard at Danny, but didn't try to speak.

"You mad that I didn't go on three?" Danny asked. "You would have tensed up and made it hurt more." *Yank.* "I know, you're even more mad now. But trust me, kid, it hurts worse when you—" *yank* "—know it's coming."

He spoke from personal experience on that one. Having the shrapnel pulled out of his leg from the day of the car accident was one of the worst medical procedures of his life. The doctor doing it had counted to three before he removed each and every single piece, and Danny had tensed up each and every time.

Ghostly wisps of a helicopter's whir tickled at his eardrums, so faint he thought he'd imagined it at first. Gradually, though, it grew louder and a medevac chopper dropped to the ground in the middle of the park, a short distance from the end of the line of booths.

"Finally," Camilla said with relief. "I've never been so happy to see a helicopter in my life."

He murmured an agreement as he taped gauze over the wounds he'd just pulled the wood slivers from. "That should help a little," he told their patient. "But don't touch the rest of them, okay?"

Sanitizing his hands yet again, he grabbed fresh gloves and moved out to meet the flight paramedics. He sent Rick with them first. They had him on a stretcher and were back in the helicopter taking off within minutes.

Hopefully, there were more on the way. More medical personnel, something. Camilla had looked so relieved to see that chopper. Hopefully, she wouldn't be disappointed at the size of the rescue crew.

"We need a doctor over here," someone shouted. "We can't move this guy and he's in bad shape."

He and Camilla both grabbed an armful of supplies and headed in that direction.

They found a man with the majority of a booth collapsed on him. His lower half was pinned beneath the wooden structure and his abdomen was flayed open. Danny had to bite back a curse. They were going to need another medevac chopper for sure.

He sank down on his knees and started assessing. Airway seemed clear as the man was able to breathe, although the breathing was ragged. Circulation was going to be a problem, with the amount of weight crushing the guy's lower extremities, though. He was going to be at real risk for crush syndrome. He pressed as much gauze as he had to the wound and secured it as best he could. It wasn't going to be more than a stopgap measure that would hopefully buy him some time to get him to hospital.

"Let's get an IV started," he said to Camilla. When he looked over at her, she'd already started to prep for that.

"I assumed you'd want that." She wiped the man's arm with an antiseptic wipe before inserting the IV needle in place, taking care not to jar him. She taped the cannula down and hung the IV bag of saline on the frame of the collapsed booth above his head.

The patient was in and out of consciousness, which was a bit of a worry. Danny wasn't sure if the man was bleeding beneath the wood that was piled on him or if it was merely pain taking him out.

"We need to stabilize him in the event of a spinal injury." He closed his eyes briefly and thought about what they could use. As a small-town clinic, they didn't keep that sort of equipment on hand. He needed a DIY replacement.

Quilts.

He hopped up and ran over to Mrs. Sutherland's booth. "I need all the quilts or blankets you can spare. And if you all could scrounge up some duct tape, that would be a huge help."

Mrs. Sutherland handed him a stack of quilts and the sparkly booth next to her pulled out a roll of shiny duct tape. He carried the armload of supplies back to his crush victim.

"Help me roll these into blocks to stabilize him with. Also, if someone could find us maybe a kid's sled or something long and flat that we can use as a makeshift backboard, that would be great."

He and Camilla quickly rolled the quilts and taped them tight to use as blocks to stabilize the patient so that they could hopefully move him. Someone ran up with a large sheet of plywood.

Danny and Camilla worked in sync, supporting the man with the rolled-up quilts and duct-taping them across him. Once they had done all they could with the quilts, they were ready to get the plywood in place.

"Okay, guys, Dr. Devereaux and I are going to gently raise him up just enough that you should be able to slide the plywood beneath him. Slow and easy, okay? On the count of three. One. Two. Three."

With the plywood in place, they eased him down onto the wood. Danny listened to his lungs again, but there was no change.

"Now we need to get this booth off him. Camilla, you and I will have to be ready to examine the lower limbs as soon as we pull him free. Watch for bleeders and fractures or dislocations."

Camilla nodded as a group of the towns-folk gathered around the damaged booth and readied themselves to lift it.

"On three." He counted down and when the booth rose, they tugged at the plywood, pulling the man free of his entrapment.

"You," Danny said, pointing at one of the men. "Run back to the first aid tent and grab the inflatable leg splints, all the ice packs you can hold, and the box labeled Miscellaneous."

Soon the man was back, nearly dropping the large armload of supplies onto the patient.

Danny quickly grabbed the leg splints and tossed one to Camilla. "Check for fractures and distal pulses."

Camilla felt one leg while he palpated the other. The ankle was extremely deformed on his side and he could feel no pulse in the foot. He slipped the leg splint under the man's leg and then carefully tugged the foot back into the vicinity of straight. A faint pulse met him for the effort. He inflated the splint and looked over to see Camilla inflating hers, as well.

"No obvious deformities," she said. "Surprising, considering all that."

The whir of a helicopter overhead was a welcome sound. He joked, "Oh, now they show up. After we've done all the hard work."

Camilla snorted. "I bet they'll take all the credit, too."

The next few hours passed in a blur as they sent patient after patient to the hospital in ambulances, medevac choppers, and even the back seats of cars. As evening drew near, the line of people waiting for care had trickled down to a slow crawl. When they hadn't seen a patient in over twenty minutes, Danny finally thought it was safe to close the first aid tent up for the night.

Sinking down on a cooler, he opened a

bottle of water and downed it in practically a single gulp. He could live the rest of his life without another day like this. Working trauma in a fully equipped medical center—that he could handle. But he'd left his days of field medicine behind when he left the Army. Or so he'd thought… The bottle in his hand started to shake as the adrenaline that had fueled him for hours wore off and all that remained were the unwanted aftereffects.

Camilla sank down on the cooler next to him, unusually quiet. She held an unopened bottle of water in her hands. Waves of exhaustion rolled off her and he felt each and every one in his own bones.

"You okay?"

She nodded slowly, but then contradicted herself. "No, I don't think I am. I'm going to have nightmares about this for weeks."

"Weeks if you are lucky. Years, more likely." Danny picked at the label on his water bottle, peeling the wrapper off slowly, as he talked to Camilla. Finally, he opened up to her a little. "Seeing people that you know with blood running down their faces, with their chests flayed open, and in obvious agony, it's not something you get over easily."

Choking back a sob, Camilla leaned her head against his shoulder. The heat of her tears soaked through his T-shirt. He slid his arm around her shoulder and just let her cry. Occasionally, he murmured a reassurance, but nothing he could say would ease the pain of seeing so many friends with traumatic injuries. He knew that from experience as deep as his soul.

He'd had the benefit of distance today. There were some familiar faces, yes, but he wasn't involved with these people on a daily basis like Camilla. It made it easier for him to push them into the role of patient and leave them there. For her, though, these people weren't just patients; they were her friends, the people she sat with at church on Sunday, and the foster kids she tutored in biology. They meant something to her, and that simple fact alone meant that staying objective and keeping a mental distance would have been impossible for her. He knew that pain. He'd had the same struggles while patching up his platoon. But worse than caring for his men had been the pain of trying to save his mom and brother and knowing he could do nothing. That had been what had broken him and sent him on that one-way ticket out of town.

He hugged her tighter, wishing he could shoulder the brunt of her pain. "It's going to be okay."

"Excuse me." A man cleared his throat. "Sorry to interrupt."

Danny looked up to see a uniformed police officer standing a few feet away. "What can I help you with?" he asked, hoping it wasn't medical care. He was wiped and Camilla was in no shape to treat any patients.

"I need to get statements from both of you for our investigation. Do you have a minute?" the officer asked. "Maybe I could start with you, sir?"

"Yeah, I'll go first," Danny offered, glancing at Camilla, who was swiping roughly at her tear-stained face and trying to gather her composure. If treating neighbors had hurt her this badly, how would she react if she ever lost a loved one? Was it fair to her to have her fall in love with him again? Danny swallowed hard. What was he doing to her?

CHAPTER ELEVEN

"THIS ALL HAS to be a horrible dream, a nightmare, really," Camilla muttered to herself as she cleaned up the first aid tent. She boxed up the few supplies that remained to go back to the clinic. It all fit in a single cardboard box that she could carry with one hand. Fidget outweighed the box of leftover medical bits. A handful of colorful children's bandages, one box of antiseptic, bottles of sunscreen, and some packets of pain reliever were all that was left unused.

And she'd teased Danny that he'd overprepared.

Never again would she fault him for wanting to have more supplies than they ever expected to use. In fact, she'd probably bring all the supplies they possessed to any events they attended in the future.

But, oh, man, was she going to need to place a massive supply order the next day. She might have to run out and stock up with what limited supplies she could get at the drugstore just to see them through until her supplier could get the clinic replenished.

She carried the little box over to the clinic herself and set it on the floor of the mostly empty supply closet. Repeating to herself, "It's all gonna be okay, it's all gonna be okay," she tried hard not to burst into tears again. Hopefully, her little mantra would keep the nightmares away, because the horror and destruction of the past eight hours still dogged her every breath.

Camilla liked to think of herself as a level-headed person, a strong and capable woman who kept her head in an emergency. But even the strongest had their limits and hers had been breached today. She wasn't prone to drama, but surely a few tears were warranted, given the day's events.

She took a moment to wash her face and hands before changing into the spare outfit she kept at the clinic. As a family practitioner, she'd learned to keep a change of clothes handy because if you didn't, it was guaranteed that a puking patient would make you wish you had. Her old clothes she tossed in the biohazard bag. She didn't want to know what was on them and she wasn't risking taking them home with her.

That done, she walked back over to the first aid tent, which was completely empty. Glancing around, she saw no sign of Danny, who'd been giving his statement. Where could he have gone?

No sign of Officer Shea, either. Figuring they'd eventually come here to look for her, she sat down and put her throbbing feet up. What a day!

While she waited, she pulled her phone out and called Alma to check on Maddie. Alma told her that Maddie was physically okay, but had cried herself to sleep over seeing her friends injured. Most of all, the girl had been worried that Alma and Dave wouldn't want to adopt her anymore. Camilla hadn't even thought about that being a possibility, but Alma had assured her that Maddie's choice of friends hadn't changed their minds about making her a permanent part of their family. Soon she would need to talk to Maddie about her the people she chose to spend her time with, but for now, sleep was the best thing for her. Alma and Camilla chatted a few more minutes about Maddie until Camilla saw Officer Shea walking up. She ended the call with a promise to check on Maddie the next day.

"Dr. Devereaux, is now a better time for your statement?" Officer Shea asked, pulling a small notebook and pen out of his uniform pocket.

"It's as good as it's going to get after the day I've had." She patted her hand on the wooden counter where she sat. "You don't mind if I sit, do you? It's been a long day and I am exhausted."

"Of course, no problem at all." Officer Shea flipped through his little book until he found a blank page and scrawled her name across the top in black ink. "I'd like to ask you a few questions about today, starting with, did you see what happened?"

Camilla recounted what she knew, which wasn't much.

Shea closed his notebook and shoved it roughly back into his pocket. "You've corroborated what I've been hearing. Teenagers messing with the dang fireworks. Serves 'em right if they have lasting scars, after they hurt half the town and traumatized the rest."

She raised an eyebrow at him and he colored under her scrutiny. That was a harsh statement to make, particularly in regards to young people.

"I mean, I don't wish none of them any permanent harm or nothing. But they should have a reminder of what they done wrong, don't ya think?" Shea held his ground on his opinion, even if he softened it slightly.

With a sigh, she nodded at him, too tired to argue that they were young and had made a stupid mistake. "Do you know where Dr. Owens went?"

"No, ma'am, I sure don't." Shea nodded and took a step back. "You have a good night, ma'am."

Ma'am? How old did he think she was? She was only a few years older than Officer Shea and he wanted to call her *ma'am*? She hopped down from the counter shaking her head. Sometimes Southern manners made her want to hurt someone.

She pulled her phone off and sent a text to Danny.

His reply came quickly.

I'm sorry, but I need some time.

Her heart raced as she processed those words. He needed time? Because of what had just happened? Because of her? Because he was leaving town again and never coming back?

She sucked in a deep breath and sent him a single word reply. If Danny was gone, then she might as well call it a night and go take care of Fidget. Her poor puppy was probably about to piddle all over her crate after this long.

As she walked home, she noticed the town was unusually quiet. Yards were empty, and so were the streets. She couldn't blame her neighbors for wanting to be safe and sound within the walls of their homes. That was certainly where she wanted to be, even if she didn't want to be alone.

When she walked up the drive to her house, some of the stress melted away, because she knew that in this house, she was safe. She spared a glance at the gate to the backyard to make sure it was latched before she went up on the porch. Another night like last night was beyond her current energy level and emotional capacity.

Fidget started barking as soon as she unlocked the front door. "I'm coming, Fidget," she called out. When she opened the crate, the little black-and-white dog darted out between her feet and started running in a circle around the kitchen, yapping her little head off.

Camilla didn't even bother shushing the dog, and let her get her energy out. Unlocking the back door, she let Fidget out and stepped out on the porch to sit and watch while her dog ran laps around the yard.

When Fidget had done her business and gotten tired, she came back up on the porch and hopped up in Camilla's lap. Camilla hugged the little dog close, burying her face in the mutt's shaggy fur. For years, she'd prided herself on her collected demeanor, the key to which was having a good purge every so often. Usually, that took the shape of a sad movie or book. Today, the explosion of fireworks and resulting trauma had forced that purge. Or rather, the aftermath had, because once the adrenaline had left, all that remained was a desperate need to cry.

"Oh, Fidget, I can't even tell you what a day I had." Tears fell unimpeded from her eyes and dampened the dog's fur. "I don't want to even speak of it out loud, it's so awful. And Danny may...he may not be coming back."

Flopping forward on the empty bed, Danny punched his pillow and bunched it up under his head. He'd taken the coward's way out in leaving without speaking to Camilla.

She'd texted him. A single word.

Goodbye.

It had a finality to it that sent an ache down through his core. Somehow, he'd ignored every light flashing a warning of dangerous roads ahead and had pushed forward until his lips were pressed firmly to Camilla's and her curves were against his body, tempting him to want things he had no business wanting. What had he been thinking?

He *knew* Camilla should have been off-limits. He'd left once to protect her from himself. Not much had changed, so why he thought another attempt at their doomed relationship had made sense was escaping him at the moment.

But a few months back, Old Man Jenkins had gotten him thinking about the what-ifs… And the sweet kisses he'd shared with Camilla had only doubled the ante on that gamble.

What if he'd never ended things with her? If he hadn't, they would have been long married by now. Maybe he'd have given in to her wishes to settle in Greenbriar. Or maybe he'd have gotten her to consider somewhere else. Maybe Boston, but Camilla was a Southern girl through and through, so most likely they'd have stayed somewhere in the South. They could have had children. It had been something they'd talked about—with plans to have both biological and adopted. A picture of a little girl, Camilla's mini-me, popped up in his mind and made him smile.

Those hypothetical children could still happen. It wasn't too late, at least not from a biological standpoint, but the worry that she would never really trust him enough to build a future with him, to have a family with him sat heavy on his heart.

What if he hurt her again? Worse than he had before.

And that was the biggest what-if, right there. And, to be truthful, the most probable outcome. He could see in her eyes that she was falling for him a bit more each day.

He sighed.

Nothing had really changed from eight years ago. He could end up hurting her again. Somehow that felt like fact. He had a lot of soul-searching to do if he was going to keep pursuing a relationship with her, starting with finding ways to make sure his darkness didn't seep into her light. He hadn't been able to protect his mother and Robby. He'd let them down when they needed him most. They'd died and no police report saying the drunk driver was at fault could completely absolve his guilt. He should have swerved.

He couldn't be trusted to love someone.

A man was meant to protect his family. Not get them killed.

He rolled to his back and grunted in frustration. But being alone was getting harder and harder with each day that passed. He didn't want to wake up to an empty house. The silence and isolation had long grown old. He wanted so much more.

But it wasn't just his own heart he'd be risking.

Physically at least, Camilla still wanted him as much as he wanted her. That much he could be sure of. Knowing that meant making some changes to his life that he wasn't certain he wanted to make. Namely, if he wanted to be with Camilla, it would mean staying in Greenbriar for good. She'd never leave this town now.

If he went to her house tonight, then that would be it.

A commitment that he had to be completely sure of.

With his mind racing, Danny gave up on the idea of sleep. He got out of bed and went to the kitchen table, where he pulled out his journal. He opened the leather cover and flipped to the first blank page. Putting thoughts on paper had been one of the strongest coping methods he'd found. The act of writing his stresses down acted as a purge, letting him see his situations more objectively.

He'd been journaling since his time in the hospital, handed his first notebook by the therapist assigned to his case. Through the years he'd filled a dozen or more notebooks of varying sizes, but the fact remained that it was a cathartic endeavor for him. He'd carried a notebook with him in the pocket of his ACUs through multiple deployments and field assignments.

The nib of his pen scratched against the paper as he got into the flow of writing, allowing his thoughts to pour out onto the page. Concern that, whatever she said, Camilla might never fully forgive him for the past ate up a large chunk of his writing. He filled multiple pages with his insecurities and worries before he'd expelled enough emotions that rational thought seemed possible. Then another tidbit of Mr. Jenkins's advice hit him—the need to forgive himself.

Danny sighed.

Slipping the cap on his pen, he left it across the page as a bookmark for when he revisited those thoughts with fresh eyes later. Getting that little bit of distance usually helped him gain a lot of perspective over the thoughts he'd inked and allowed him to make better decisions. But forgiveness still felt so far away.

He pushed up from the table and went outside to sit on the dock. With his feet dangling just above the water, he watched the bright colors of the sunset spread across the water.

His mother had always loved the sunsets over the lake. The place had been bought as a weekend getaway, but they'd spent most of the summers out here. He and Robby had shared the tiny loft while his mom and dad had the sole bedroom, but it hadn't felt crowded. Probably because they spent so much time outside, either on the dock or on the water.

Camilla had been a little slow to warm to his mom, but his mom had refused to give up. She'd taken to Camilla from the moment they met. When he'd proposed, his mom had cried big fat tears of joy. She'd have probably kicked his butt all over Greenbriar if she'd known how badly he'd ended up hurting Camilla.

But that was what he did. He hurt people.

Camilla was better off without him. And he was better off alone.

The decision should have made him feel lighter, like a burden had been lifted from his shoulders. Instead, it felt like an anchor had been dropped on his soul. As the night settled in and darkness replaced the cascade of colors, a darkness settled over Danny, as well.

He deserved this pain.

This was his true penance. It was the end of May. He had two more months to finish out the conditions attached to his father's will. Then he could leave for Boston on August 1 and never have to see Camilla's beautiful face again.

CHAPTER TWELVE

WHEN MORNING ROLLED around without a single word from Danny, Camilla's heart filled with dread. They still had two more months on the agreement before they could inherit the medical practice and she could buy him out.

She let out a shaky breath.

Those two months might as well be an eternity. Not that she'd have to worry about seeing him every day. He'd taken the easy way out once by leaving town and he probably had done so again.

She closed Fidget in her cage and walked to the clinic alone. Each step felt like trudging through waist-deep mud as she made her way toward the dream that would shortly be snatched away from her. When she got there, she lovingly traced her fingers over her name on the glass. What would take its place when the clinic closed? Or would it sit empty like the old hardware store?

When she went to unlock the door, the knob turned freely beneath her hand. A ripple of panic ran through her. Had she forgotten to lock it yesterday? Her mind had been such a mess that it was possible.

Cautiously, she opened the door and stepped inside.

Danny sat at the front desk, typing away at the computer. He looked up and some of the color drained from his face. He nodded and returned his eyes to the screen.

If that was how he wanted to play this, she could pretend nothing had happened, too. She tried to keep her chin up and refused to glance his way again as she moved past him to her office. Somehow, she resisted the urge to slam the door.

Sinking down into her chair, Camilla tried not to cry. Danny being here was wholly unexpected. She'd thought he'd have had his truck packed and been halfway back to Boston by now. Instead, he was here at work acting like he hadn't just ripped her heart out and stomped on it for the second time.

But this time was far crueler, as he had stuck around to witness her collapse.

Camilla swallowed hard.

She wouldn't give him the pleasure of seeing her crack. Straightening her posture, she rose to her feet and went to the supply closet. The clinic was in desperate need of supplies and she needed to take inventory first.

"Camilla," he said from behind her. "Can we talk?"

"What's to talk about?" She shrugged, refusing to turn and look at him. She'd always had a harder time hiding her true emotions from him. He could see through the facade she put up easier than anyone else. But Danny had wedged himself into her heart, getting closer to her than anyone else ever had. It was that closeness that let him read her so easily.

"I already made a supply list."

"I'll make my own."

Danny snorted. "You don't have to be so stubborn about this. Why make more work for yourself? Is it just to spite me? Well, honey, I'm still here. You are stuck with me for another two months whether you like it or not."

"Whether I like it or not?" She spun around, anger pulsing through her veins. "Let me tell you something. I'm getting about tired of you coming into my life and using me for your own amusement and then tossing me aside when things get serious. I would never treat you the way you have treated me. Just because you're scared doesn't mean you can take that out on me."

"Scared?" Danny scoffed. "Who said I was scared?"

"No one had to say it. It's written on your every action. You are scared of commitment. You are scared to let anyone close. Scared to love."

"I'm not scared." His eyes flashed with anger, but beneath the anger, she saw the hurt her words had caused him.

"Okay, then. You're not scared. Then answer me this one thing…why are you running again?" Raising an eyebrow at him, she crossed her arms over her chest and tapped one toe on the floor impatiently. "I'm waiting."

Rather than answer, Danny spun and stomped away.

She called after him, "And you said you weren't running scared."

When she heard the clinic door slam shut behind him, she briefly worried she might have pushed him too far, and that she'd put her future at the clinic at risk, but she had to stand up for herself. The first time Danny had left her, she'd had no chance to tell him how she felt. This time was different. She wasn't going to take this without a fight.

Danny drove out to the lake house determined to get out of Greenbriar and away from Camilla as fast as possible. He didn't have to stick around and listen to her accusing him of things that just weren't true. They could just sell the practice outright. He'd planned to stay in town so that in two months they could divide the practice between them legally, but if she wanted to push him away, he'd go.

"Who does she think she is, calling me scared?" he muttered to himself as he packed. He started throwing his things into laundry baskets and anything else he could find that would hold his belongings. He loaded the back seat of his truck as he filled the containers. The sooner he could get out of town, the better he'd feel.

"Scared to love," he said with a snort of disbelief. "How can Camilla think I'm scared to love when I'm just trying to protect her."

He pulled an old family picture off the wall. His college-aged face stared back at him standing next to his parents and brother. Camilla had taken the photo out on the dock with the sunset behind them. It had been his mom's favorite photo of them.

Carrying the framed picture with him, he walked out onto the dock. That day had been one of the happiest he could remember. He'd proposed to Camilla that very evening, right on this very dock. He ran his finger over each smiling face in the photo.

Every person in that picture wore a genuine smile beamed straight at the woman holding the camera—Camilla. His parents had been enamored with her. Robby had the most massive crush on her from day one, but he'd soon gotten over that and considered her the sister he'd never had. They'd all have been so disappointed with him for running away from her again. His dad had been extremely vocal about it the first time. Now that Danny was trying to do it again, he could imagine the lectures his father would be giving him about not running scared from the love of his life.

"I'm not scared to love?"

What he'd meant as a statement to confirm his own thoughts came out as a question. He didn't want to hurt anyone else he loved. That didn't make him scared.

Or did it?

He closed his eyes and it was Camilla's face that flashed through his thoughts. She was the first person he thought of when he woke each morning, and the last person he thought of each night before he fell asleep.

So why was he running away from her?

She was right. He was running scared. He

was the world's biggest idiot and he needed to find a way to fix this.

Now, how did he make it up to her?

He had some work to do.

And he knew just where to start.

CHAPTER THIRTEEN

WHEN THE GATE OPENED, Camilla looked over in panic. Seeing Danny cautiously step through the gate was not what she'd expected. Thankfully, he was careful not to let Fidget out.

"What all do you have there?" She tried to avoid just flat out asking him *why* he was there.

"I went to the store to get that length of chain and a padlock to secure your gate for you. I promised you that I'd secure it so that we didn't have any more escapees."

"We?" she asked, swallowing down her heart that had just filled with hope and lodged itself in her throat.

"I also brought you this." He slowly climbed the steps to the back porch and held something out to her. "I never imagined I'd show this to you, or even a therapist, to be honest. And maybe today isn't the best time. I'm not sure, but I do think you need to read it at some point. I don't expect you to dive in tonight and read every page before sunrise, though."

She took the leather-bound notebook from his outstretched hand. The patina on the leather said it had been well used. "A journal?"

"There are two inserts in there. One is my first journal that begins at the time I was in the hospital and goes through our breakup and my enlistment. The other is the most recent, covering the time I've been back in Greenbriar. The ones in the middle are probably not as beneficial, but maybe I'll show you those, as well, sometime if you are interested." He sat down next to her and took her hand in his. The porch light highlighted his solemn expression. She could see that whatever he was about to say was serious and truthful. "Someday, I want you to read this. It's not a graphic recollection of the accident or my time in the Army, nothing like that. It's more of an account of my thoughts and feelings."

"Are you sure you want me to read it?" Even as she asked, Camilla held her breath because she desperately wanted to understand where his mind was at, during the time of their breakup. She caressed the journal reverently, knowing that Danny had handed her a private piece of his soul and entrusted her with the knowledge contained within its pages. The trust he showed in allowing her access to it made her feel honored. He wasn't running away. In fact, he was finally opening up to her, which couldn't help but bring forth the slightest bit of optimism.

He nodded. Sighed loudly, and then nodded again, almost as if he was reassuring himself that it was okay. "Yeah, I think it's important for us moving forward that you do. Not going to say that it's not triggering a little anxiety, but yeah, I want you to read it."

"Thank you for trusting me enough to show me." She thought it important for her to acknowledge what a big step he'd taken in coming here. To reveal his innermost thoughts, particularly those from such a tumultuous time in his life, had to be hard. She scanned his face, reading his expression and looking at his body language. His knee bounced up and down quickly, an outward sign of his inward anxiety. "It means a lot to me," she said. "But if you need to change your mind, I do understand."

"No. You should read it."

"Not if it's going to upset you." As much as she was dying to open that front cover and absorb the words that would be written in

Danny's familiar scrawl, she needed to determine that it wasn't going to hurt him more than it helped her.

He shrugged, but rather than looking at her, his gaze was focused out somewhere midway up her back fence. His expression remained blank, emotions locked away.

"Not if it's going to upset you," Camilla repeated.

Without looking at her, he said softly, "If I want you to trust me, I have to be willing to trust you. You can read it."

"I appreciate that. If it's anything like the emotional nightmare we just went through, and I can only imagine it was worse since you were dealing with losing your immediate family, then it's no wonder you were such a mess. My life wasn't in danger, I wasn't injured, and I'm certain that I'll have nightmares from the festival for a long time to come."

"And if you do, I'll be right here to walk you through them. I won't let you shoulder that burden alone." The conviction in his eyes spoke directly to her soul. "I'm done running."

She sighed. "I really wish I could believe that."

"Babe, if I have to spend the rest of my life making this up to you, I will. Camilla, I love you. I've always loved you. Even when I was too scared to let myself love anyone, you were the only woman I thought about."

In that moment, the way he looked at her… oh, it set her heart racing. Bottom line was that she loved this man, too. She'd loved him from the time she was a mere wisp of a girl on the cusp of womanhood and she'd love him until she left this world and could love no more.

"You want some coffee?"

Caffeine was much needed if they were going to have the type of discussion he expected them to be having from the seriousness of her expression. After his sudden epiphany, he knew what he wanted, and that was a future with Camilla.

"That would be great, thanks." Camilla moved past him, a wisp of her perfume carrying on the breeze that accompanied her through the doorway of his childhood home.

She moved into the kitchen area and took a seat at the table while he walked straight to the coffeepot. He'd just scooped the grounds into the basket when Camilla spoke.

"'Do I even want Camilla to forgive me?'" she quoted.

His hands shook as he started the coffee and turned to face her.

"When did you start…?" She trailed off, gesturing toward the journal.

"I know the entries should be dated, but that was right after we broke up." He shrugged. "The therapist I saw a few times suggested I start writing one."

He sank down into the chair across from hers, but kept his focus tightly on the polished wooden tabletop. It wasn't necessarily that he was embarrassed about keeping a journal, but the contents of it were so raw and personal that it felt like she'd ripped a Band-Aid off a gaping wound in his soul by reading even that one line aloud. Having her know that she was a topic of his thoughts, enough for him to write about her, bared him to her, exposed her to the kind of hurt he'd wanted to avoid passing on. By letting her know that he cared what she thought, he had opened himself up to the pain of rejection, as well. What had he written in the lines after the heart-baring truth she'd read back to him? He struggled to recall the free-flowing words he'd practically bled out onto the page. Most of what he'd said about her was positive, he thought, but the fear lingered that she'd read an intimate detail he wasn't fully ready to share.

Camilla's gentle fingers covered his hand, slowly, cautiously, like she thought he might reject her touch. "I'm glad you are seeing someone, or have seen someone at least."

He gave a slight nod. Camilla was so perceptive. He had always said she knew him better than he knew himself.

"Good. Does the journaling help?"

He nodded again.

"That's really good to hear. I'm so happy that you've found a way to cope. I've read studies about how many psychologists were using expressive writing as a type of ongoing therapy. If I remember correctly, they were looking at how it could be beneficial for other illnesses, as well, since that sort of private reflection allows them to sort through the personal grief of their reality and helps them to process it with deeper understanding. Is that how you are using it?"

"Yes." The curtness of his answer sat at odds with the soft tones Camilla had spoken in.

Her fingers moved across his, clasping their fingers together. "I'd ask why you were unsure you wanted to be forgiven by me, but if I had to hazard a guess, it's because you don't feel like you deserve to be. Maybe you haven't yet forgiven yourself?"

He couldn't even bring himself to nod that time as she cut straight to the core of his problem. Just like in the past, Camilla saw through him and knew exactly what he was thinking, what he was dealing with. That uncanny ability to see his truth, no matter his words or outward actions, had been a large part of why he'd pushed her away. She'd have absorbed so much of his pain, trying to help him, that she would have lost herself in the process.

She paused, giving him a chance to speak, but when he remained quiet, she continued, "This seems to be making you uncomfortable, but I'll just say, there's nothing to forgive."

Jerking, he brought his gaze up to meet hers. There was so much to forgive; how could she even think that? His brow wrinkled as he tried to come up with the right words to argue that statement.

With the bluntness he'd always loved, Camilla said, "Maybe I should phrase it this way—there's nothing left to forgive. How do you see us moving forward from here?"

Tightening his fingers around hers, he leaned forward and brushed his lips over the pulse point at her wrist. "I'm worried that what I want will be exactly what you don't need."

"I'm a big girl now, Danny, and I haven't

needed you to protect me from anyone in a very long time."

But who will protect you from me? ran through Danny's thoughts, but he shoved that insecurity back and focused on the fact that the woman he still loved was in front of him, and willing to talk to him, even if he had messed up so badly in a thousand different ways. Since he'd ended their engagement, he'd been floating through life making no meaningful connections, allowing no one to get close. That was no way to live and he didn't want to do it anymore.

This wasn't a game. He couldn't press Pause or start over if he made a mistake. This wasn't casual dating, not for him. This was his entire future risked on convincing one beautiful woman to trust in his flawed and imperfect self.

Even a few short months ago, the idea of spending half a year in Greenbriar had felt like a heavy chain wrapped around his neck, choking the life from him, but now it symbolized a rebirth. In Greenbriar, and with Camilla, he could find the Danny that had been lost all those years ago and become the man he'd always intended to be.

He'd sure as heck never planned to become the grumpy old bachelor who people shied away from out of fear that he'd bite their heads off. Somehow, he'd always thought he'd be a lot like his dad, the type of man that people looked up to and came to whenever they had a problem, medical or not. He had a long way to go if he wanted to be that man, though. Maybe too far.

And he wanted to do it with Camilla at his side. He and Camilla were meant to be together. She was his future. That much he was sure of.

"Your forgiveness of all the pain I caused you is more proof of your strength. I'm here because of stubbornness. Camilla, you are the strongest woman I've ever known and I'm sorry I couldn't see that sooner."

"You know I need to read this right now." She waved the journal at him slightly.

"I didn't mean tonight…" He trailed off when he noticed the obstinate set to her jaw. Briefly, he considered arguing, but then she crossed her arms and stared until he backed down. Knowing better than to try to stop her when she'd put her mind to something, he shrugged and made the woman some coffee while she carried the journal off through the house.

When he followed a few minutes later with two mugs of steaming coffee, he found her snuggled up on the couch under a teal throw blanket with her nose buried in his journal. He sat the mug on the table next to her and she flashed a faint smile in his direction before her eyes focused back on the page.

He sank down on the opposite end of the couch and she tucked her feet under his thigh. Sipping at the steaming mug of black coffee, he reflected back on his last year. If anyone had asked him twelve months ago where he saw himself, the last place Danny would have said he would have been was cuddled up on the couch in his childhood home with the one who "got away." Never thought he'd truly consider this town his home. He'd spent so much of his youth counting down the days until he could get out of there that he'd never once imagined coming home to Greenbriar to stay.

Everyone who knew him would have put money on him staying in Boston or moving to another big city. They'd have said he liked shallow people and even shallower relationships. Some might have called him an adrenaline junkie or a rolling stone. And while that might have been true even a few months ago, now they would be all kinds of wrong. The things that man wanted no longer appealed.

Thanks to Camilla, his entire plan for the future had shifted.

Danny was not only in his hometown, but planning to spend the rest of his life here. Assuming Camilla agreed to marry him. *Again*. While he'd occasionally fantasized occasionally about Camilla's return to his life, he'd always thought of her coming to him in whatever city he was living in at that time. Returning to Greenbriar had never factored into any of his fantasies.

But here he was and, excluding the unusual horrors from earlier in the week, he was happier than he'd been in years. And it was all thanks to the woman at his side, and her wonderful, forgiving heart.

Camilla adjusted her position and the movement sent the soft scent of her perfume wafting through the air to tickle at his nose. Every now and then, her breath would catch and that little noise would send his heart on a jog, as the irrational worry of that page being the one that sent her running for the hills crept into his mind. But she would simply pause to wipe away a few tears and continue reading.

When she got to the pages where he had been contemplating suicide, she sat up and hugged him so tight that he couldn't breathe.

Her tears soaked his shirt, and in the quiet room, her sobs sounded painfully loud.

"Before you ask, I no longer feel that way and I haven't for a long time. That was years ago, before I joined the Army." He should have warned her about that part. Using his thumbs, he brushed the tears away from her cheeks. Hopefully, this would be the last of the pain he'd cause her from his actions over eight years ago. "You know I think I've seen you cry more this week than in the entire time I've known you?"

"Maybe I'm just finally opening up more myself." Camilla kissed his cheek, but bravely dove back in to her reading. The suicidal thoughts had been the worst of it, so the rest should be easier on her, he hoped. While she read, he kept himself busy with checking out all the changes she'd made to the house he'd grown up in. Somehow, she'd turned it into even more of a home. Within these walls, he didn't feel the creeping darkness. Even while she was reading the journal where he'd poured so many emotions out in his messy script, he didn't feel panicked or have the urge to snatch it from her hands. To say he had zero anxiety about her deep dive into his emotional past might be overselling it, but he wasn't on the verge of a panic attack at least.

When she turned the last page and flipped the journal closed, his breath came a bit easier. He waited impatiently after she finished reading, to hear her thoughts, her opinions, to see if it helped her with the whys behind his reasons for ending their engagement, to hear if she'd ever fully forgive him. With how entangled his reasons were, with his confused mindset at the time, it was important for her to know what kind of condition he was in. But for what seemed like an eternity, she sat holding his hand, staring down at their interlaced fingers.

Did she really forgive him? Did she hate him? Was she trying to think up a polite way to tell him to get out of her house and out of her life? His heart couldn't take much more waiting.

Finally, she looked up at him. Questions filled her eyes. Her fingers grazed along the line of his jaw, so light and tender. "So, when you said you were not cut out to be a husband…?"

"I could have married you and gone through the motions, but I was so lost in my head that I know for sure I'd have made us both miserable." Breathing deep and slow, he measured his words. This was a loaded topic and hard to vocalize. "I thought you were better off without me. At the time, I didn't see it as running away. I saw it as protecting you by removing a dangerous element from your life."

"You thought you were dangerous to me?" Shaking her head at him, she countered, "You were wrong. And I would have told you myself if I thought that I was better off without you."

He wasn't surprised by her statement. Not really. Camilla was a strong and proud woman who knew her own mind. Somehow, he'd lost sight of that fact and look where it had landed them. He'd have to try harder to remember exactly who she was, going forward.

"I know that now." He grimaced, considering how he wanted to approach the rest of this conversation. He slouched back on the couch and blew out a breath. "Don't hate me for saying this, but I wasn't sure you were strong enough to face what I was dealing with."

She raised an eyebrow, calling him on the falsehood he'd just blatantly spewed without thought. Silence hung heavy between them until he revised his statement.

"Scratch that… Truthfully, I convinced myself that you weren't strong enough, that I was toxic to you, and I let those false assumptions lead me down the road to utter stupidity." He reached out and let his fingertips touch her cheek. Irritation still glittered in the depths of her blue eyes. She was not going to make this easy on him. "It's not an excuse, but an explanation that hopefully helps you understand why I did what I did."

"You went so far down the road to stupidity that I think you set up camp there." The ghostly hint of a smile landed on her lips. He added another item to the list of things he loved about her—the way she tried to hide her smile when she was snarky, but was never really successful.

Her words were probably meant to lighten up the conversation that had moved deep into the heavy zone, but he wasn't finished explaining how he'd gone so far off course with her.

"You're right. Your strength is a force of nature. I shouldn't have doubted you, because even after I destroyed all your hopes and dreams, you picked yourself up. You made a life here without me. You kept standing and you accomplished the plans you set in motion all those years ago. You have a successful medical practice—don't think I didn't hear that you kept it going alone while Dad was sick. I was lost, though. The demons in my head outweighed my confidence in all aspects of my life. With all the negative thoughts, my insecurities became stronger than my common sense. And I wasn't strong enough at that moment to fight for us. I was exhausted from just fighting for myself. It wasn't until I came back here that I started seeing what I was missing out on with my self-imposed isolation."

"I know." She held the journal up and gave it a shake for emphasis. "This gave me so much insight. Reading firsthand what you were dealing with emotionally… Man, that was heartbreaking. You should be proud of how you fought those demons and didn't let them win."

Fidget ran over, and after a couple of false starts, managed to hop up on the couch next to them. She jumped in Danny's lap, sniffed his cheek and then snorted in his face. "Aww, come on, really, Fidget?" Despite his exasperation at the dog's unhygienic actions, she'd really grown on him. "What's next, sneezing in my eye?"

"She only snorts or sneezes in the faces of people she loves," Camilla said indulgently, rubbing the little dog's ear. "She's been kind of a mama's girl and doesn't like just anyone, you know."

"You think she'll like me as her daddy?"

His heart pounded half out of his chest, but it was too late to take the words back now. He should have planned something romantic, taken her for a moonlit stroll, or out for a fancy dinner in the city. She deserved more than a blurted proposal via a dog, but it was too late to recall those words now.

Camilla gaped at him. For an unbearably long beat, she sat staring at him, completely motionless. Finally, she blinked rapidly before asking, "What are you saying, Danny?"

He stood and pulled the jeweler's box out of his pocket.

"Oh…" she breathed the single syllable. Her gaze darted from the black velvet box in his hand to his eyes and back. Tears welled up in her eyes, but the smile that graced her face was bright enough to power the town.

"Camilla Devereaux, I asked you this once before and your answer then was yes. I'm hoping you'll say yes again tonight. If you do, I promise I'll never give you reason to regret it." Dropping to one knee, Danny asked her the most important question a man could ask his woman. "Will you marry me?"

"Yes," she said, her voice solid and unwavering. She held her hand out for him to slip the ring on her finger. "I'd love nothing more than to marry you."

"This is going right back where it belongs," he said as he took the ring out of the box. The diamond slid onto her finger, a perfect fit, as it always had been. "I never should have taken it off your finger in the first place."

With that done, he pressed his lips to hers and poured all the love and desire he felt for her into that embrace. They clung together, entangled until they had to come up for air.

Emotion clogged his throat, making his voice gruff. "Hard to believe that only a few short months ago I thought you were out of my life for good. So much has changed."

"I know." She smiled, but then a seriousness passed over her expression. Far too weighty for minutes after a proposal.

"What's wrong?" His mind raced as he tried to problem-solve how she'd gone from tears of happiness to serious and morose in the space of seconds.

With a sigh, she gave him a sad little smile. "I suppose we will have to set up a visitation schedule for when you go back to Boston."

So that was the problem? She still thought he was leaving. Relief coursed through him when he knew it was something so easily remedied.

Tucking a lock of hair behind her ear,

Danny said, "I have something for you. Don't move."

He ran out to his truck and came back with a folder. He handed it to her without another word.

When she opened it, she looked down at the legal papers inside and asked, "When do you leave?" Her voice sounded a little choked.

"That wasn't the reaction I expected."

"I appreciate the gesture. It means the world to me that you would just give me your half of the clinic."

"But…"

She sighed. "I wanted a real marriage where we were together every night. But I suppose I'll learn to like the long-distance thing as long as we are together."

"I never said I was going back to Boston."

"Aren't you?" Hope blossomed in her eyes.

"Nah. I have everything I need and I think it's time I put down some roots right here in Greenbriar. Have to admit, this place has grown on me." He grinned. "Besides, Greenbriar needs a trauma surgeon for the new medevac station that's going to be set up here in the fall. Boston would be a little too much of a commute."

Camilla closed her eyes and a single tear trekked down her cheek. When he wiped it away, she let out a little chuckle and shook her head. She bit her lower lip and tried to hide a smile. Unsuccessfully, yet again.

"Tell me what you're thinking?" he asked, curious to know what amused her about him staying in Greenbriar.

Her lips twitched before a full smile graced her face. "Just wondering if your dad was looking down right now saying 'I told you so' and grinning from ear to ear."

"As much effort as he put into orchestrating my reunion with you, Dr. Devereaux, I think you could put money on it." Danny pulled her in close, his chest shaking with laughter. With Camilla tucked safely in his arms, he let out a deep sigh and looked up.

"Thanks, Dad. This one time, I'm thankful you meddled in my life."

Five years later

"Everybody that comes to my princess tea party birthday is going to wear a pretty princess dress. Even you, Daddy!"

"A princess tea party?" Danny said, his voice filled with horror. "Are you sure you want a princess tea party for your birthday? We could do pirates or a bouncy house?"

Camilla struggled to hide her laughter.

Their almost four-year-old daughter had wrapped Danny around her little finger within a minute of her birth, but having him wear a princess dress might stretch beyond the hold she had on her daddy.

"There will be no pirates at my party," Lindy insisted. "Only princesses."

The resignation in his voice was almost too much for Camilla. "But Daddy's not a princess, honey."

Lindy tilted her head and gave him the smile that usually got her way, and Camilla decided to step in before her husband ended up in a ball gown at the whim of his daughter. That little girl could talk him into about anything when she batted those eyelashes at him.

"If you are a princess, that makes Daddy a king. And kings can't be seen in a dress." She tapped Lindy on the nose playfully. "You wouldn't want a big ol' dragon to come in and think our kingdom had no king, would you?"

Their little girl considered Camilla's question carefully. Camilla could practically see the gears turning while Lindy considered that possibility and she really hoped she'd made things better, not worse. Danny might end up in a dragon costume instead of a frilly dress.

Finally, Lindy shook her head. "No, I don't want a dragon. Okay, Daddy, the king can wear pants, but everyone else has to wear a princess dress." She skipped off to chase Fidget around the yard.

Danny wrapped his arms around Camilla. "I'm so outnumbered here. Thank you for stepping in there. I thought for sure I was gonna get stuck agreeing to some fluffy pink concoction that would make me the laughing-stock of the town."

Snuggling into his embrace, Camilla laughed. "It was purely self-preservation on my part. But if you are lucky, this one will be a boy and help balance out the numbers."

Danny leaned back so that their eyes met. "Are you…?"

She nodded. Her blood work had come back to confirm what her body and the two pink lines on the home test had already told her. Their second little one was on the way.

Things had never been more perfect for her. She had a thriving medical practice, a loving husband, one healthy child, and another on the way. It was all she'd ever dreamed of.

"I'm going to be a daddy again?" Danny asked, his hand coming to rest on her still-flat stomach.

She nodded again. "What do you think?"

"I have never been happier." A wide smile

graced his handsome face. "I love you, Dr. Devereaux."

"And I love you, Dr. Owens."

* * * * *

If you enjoyed this story, check out these other great reads from Allie Kincheloe

A Nurse, a Surgeon, a Christmas Engagement

Heart Surgeon's Second Chance

Both available now!